Amendment of Life

By the same author

Catherine Aird

Amendment of Life

 St. Martin's Minotaur New York

www.minotaurbooks.com

ISBN 0-312-29080-2

First published in Great Britain by Macmillan
An imprint of Pan Macmillan Ltd.

First St. Martin's Minotaur Edition: January 2003

10 9 8 7 6 5 4 3 2 1

In Memoriam

K. W. E. G.

Amendment of Life

Chapter One

'Toss you for it?' said Pete Carter.

'It's your turn anyway,' objected Kenny Prickett.

'Not mine. I did it last Monday, remember, while you did the car park?'

Pete started to feel in his trousers' pocket for a coin. 'I know, but—'

'But', finished his friend for him, 'you don't like going in there.'

'You're dead right, I don't. It beats me why it's so blooming popular,' said Pete. He sniffed. 'Can't understand it myself.'

'People like mazes,' declared Kenny confidently. 'They queue up for ages to get in there. You can see them doing it all the time.'

'And they queue up to get out, too, mate. Don't forget that. Only you can't see them then—'

'Don't forget what goes in has to come out,' said Kenny sturdily. 'Just like what goes up has to come down.'

Pete grimaced. 'That's only if you can find your way out in the first place. It's not like you're on a straight road with signposts telling you which way to go next when you're in there.' He held up a coin. 'Come on, Kenny,' he urged. 'Live dangerously for once. Let's toss for it.'

His workmate, Kenneth Prickett, leaned against the giant industrial dustbin on wheels from which hung his brush and shovel and said, 'Oh, all right then . . . only do get on with it.'

The two workmen had just arrived at Aumerle Court to start their week's work and Monday was always their busiest day. It was the only one on which the general public were not admitted to the Court and thus the day on which a great deal of clearing up had to be done. The owners of Aumerle Court – the Pedlinge family – were careful to foster the illusion that their paying visitors were actually welcome guests and therefore liked as much as possible of the routine cleaning and tidying up to be done when that same public were not around to see the work in progress.

Pete Carter steadied a twopenny piece on his horny thumb. 'Heads you do the maze and I get to do the car park instead. Right?'

'If we don't get started pretty soon on both,' remarked Kenny pertinently, 'old Pusher Prosser'll be along wanting to know the reason why and then there'll be trouble. Big trouble. You know what he's like when he's roused, so don't let's hang about.'

Captain Jeremy Prosser was steward and agent to the Aumerle estate, and thus unhappily poised between those who wanted the work done and those who had to do it.

'You call then,' said Pete, getting ready to spin the coin up in the air.

'And none of your catching it as it comes down and turning it over in your hand, see?' said Kenny Prickett vigorously.

'Right. Call now—'

'Tails.'

'Here goes—'

Prickett shifted his heavy metal bin out of the way and watched as the twopenny piece spiralled first upwards, spun and then fell back to earth in a diminishing giro. As solemnly as a pair of cricket captains at a Test match, the two men advanced together the better to see how the coin lay on the ground.

'Tails it is,' said Pete, peering down, patently disappointed.

'Good,' said Kenny Prickett briskly, immediately starting to push his great bin in the direction of the car park. 'See you beaver time, then . . .'

'That's if I ever get out.' Pete gave a histrionic laugh. 'You realize you may never see me again, don't you?'

'Keep turning left,' advised Kenny callously.

'That's all very well, but once I go in there who knows when I'll ever come out?'

'Old Pusher Prosser will,' said his mate, taking this literally. 'He's probably timing you already if you did but know.' Everyone on the staff at Aumerle Court had soon discovered that Captain Prosser worked to the clock and that he expected everyone else to do the same.

Pete muttered exactly what Captain Prosser could do with his precious military precision, but he did it under his breath. The gentleman in question had an unnerving habit of appearing where he was least expected.

And when.

'You can do the car park next Monday,' promised Kenny, lifting the handles of his bin and beginning to trundle off towards the old stable yard, where visitors to the Court were asked to leave their vehicles, 'seeing as how it'll be your rightful turn then anyway.'

'Thanks for nothing,' said his friend, turning in the direction of the solid yew-hedge maze that lay to one side of the ancient Court.

Like other mazes of its period, it had been so positioned that those looking down from the windows at the end of the Long Gallery on the first floor could be entertained by the sight of the heads of those inside the maze struggling to get round it and regain their freedom. The fact that those above the maze – usually the ladies of the family – could themselves see the way out clearly enough when those inside couldn't presumably added to their pleasure.

'And, Pete,' called out the departing Kenny Prickett over his shoulder, 'don't forget the Captain's motto for the maze.' He grinned. 'His Monday morning one.'

Pete ground his teeth. The Captain's mottos were a

bane to everyone. They were, in fact, a thinly disguised substitute for the 'aims and objectives' principles which the good soldier had been taught at his staff college were essential to successful administration.

'"Leave no avenue unexplored",' sang out Kenny, carefully putting some distance between himself and his friend as he did so.

Exploring avenues was part of Pete's problem in this job. Even had he been able to memorize the correct route in the maze from the entrance to the exit, it would have done him no good at all. This was because he was required to tidy up all the blind alleys, nooks and crannies, and false – though promising – starts in the maze as well. And while those in the Long Gallery, scanning the maze from above, were able to relish an Olympian view of the struggles of those beneath them and could always see the easy – the only – way out, anyone actually inside the maze enjoyed no such all-encompassing view.

Not, of course, that Pete was supposed to get out of the maze as quickly as possible, unlike the visitors to Aumerle Court. He had not, after all, paid good money to go in there. Nor was there a cream tea awaiting him in the stables, which had been thoughtfully placed beside the gift shop now set up in the old laundry. Pete had to go in the maze and stay in there until the work was done – and for not very good money at all.

And then get out again.

This was Pete's complaint, too, as well as his problem. Even to the initiated, one stretch of yew hedge looked remarkably like the next and the sky was never any help at all. Pete had found that the clouds above moved with surprising speed and in all directions.

He halted as he heard Kenny call out his name. 'What is it now?'

'We could toss again next week, if you like.' Kenny Prickett gave a throaty chuckle. 'Then I might get to do the car park again. I'd have a fifty–fifty chance, wouldn't I?'

'Pete Carter's late again this week,' announced Daphne Pedlinge, adding crisply, 'And so are you, Milly.'

'Now, Miss Daphne, you shouldn't be saying that. You know I'm not. I was in your bedroom on the stroke of eight o'clock this morning, like always.'

'Push me nearer the window,' commanded Daphne Pedlinge, changing tack. 'I want to keep an eye on him.'

'Yes, Miss Daphne.' As a rule, today's carers addressed the elderly and ill more informally – Christian names were *de rigueur* in most care homes and hospitals. But Aumerle Court was neither of these things and, while undeniably elderly, Miss Pedlinge did not greatly care for this new practice.

'Nearer, Milly, please. I can't see if Pete Carter's gone in already. I don't want to miss him.'

Milly glanced at her watch as she helped to position the wheelchair. 'He'll scarcely be there yet . . . there's hardly been time for him to get across to the maze from that bothy of theirs, now has there?'

'And mind you put the brake on.'

'I haven't ever forgotten,' responded Milly cheerfully, manoeuvring Daphne Pedlinge's wheelchair into position at the end of the Long Gallery with a dexterity born of much practice, and giving it an affectionate shake, 'now have I?'

'Don't humour me, Milly.'

The woman gave a good-natured grin. 'All right, then, I'll leave you just here all day . . . where you can't see a thing.'

'No, you won't.' Miss Pedlinge's expression became positively vulpine. 'I want to watch him get lost.'

Milly suppressed any reference to what she herself felt, or, indeed, to the more modern meaning of the invitation to 'get lost'. She had been born and bred in the village of Staple St James and was thus quite accustomed to the vagaries of the Pedlinge family. Indeed, Daphne Pedlinge, a true survivor from an earlier age, had been a feature in the landscape of Milly Smithers's own life as long as she could remember.

To a little girl she had seemed kindly but awesome, and to a growing woman she had only been a friendly but distant figure, busy and much away from Aumerle Court. Then, after her elderly parents and her nephew had died, Miss Daphne had come back to take charge of Aumerle Court. That had been when the much-married woman whom Milly had then become, with all the troubles that came with the wedded state and motherhood, had found Daphne Pedlinge unfailingly approachable and helpful.

The passing years had found the boot on the other foot and it had become Milly's turn to show an equal compassion and concern.

Milly said 'Now, I ask you, is that kind, Miss Daphne? Poor Pete—'

'No,' said the old lady frankly, 'but it livens up a dull morning. And there's nothing else to look forward to today but the doctor coming.'

'He's nice, is Dr Browne,' said Milly fondly. 'I like him.'

'He can't do anything more for me, though,' said Daphne Pedlinge. 'He keeps on saying so.'

'There's not that much wrong with you,' said the woman warmly. 'All you need, Miss Daphne, are some new legs.'

'True.' Daphne Pedlinge looked down at the rug which covered a pair of arthritic, misshapen knees. 'But he hasn't got any of those in his little black bag.'

Milly propelled the wheelchair forward again and asked with genuine solicitude, 'Now, Miss Daphne, can you see all you want from here?'

'Yes, thank you, Milly.' The old lady twitched her rug. 'I'm quite all right. Now, you can go and attend to *Eurostopodus diabolicus . . .*'

'Yes, Miss Daphne.' Milly smiled dutifully at the daily joke. By now she knew that this was Latin for a bird called the Satanic-eared nightjar – and that the reference was a pun. The nightjar to which she had to attend every morning was of quite a different variety. 'Here's your bell. Just ring for me if you want anything.'

The carer had settled the wheelchair in exactly the same place – had she known it – from which the ladies of Aumerle Court of yesteryear had also diverted themselves by looking down on the maze. It had been convention, not arthritis, which had prevented those earlier gentlewomen from going outside, but they were the spiritual sisters of Daphne Pedlinge all the same. They, too, had always wanted to see what was going on in the maze, hoping for some little excitement to enliven their dull days.

Had they seen what Daphne Pedlinge saw there when she first looked down this Monday morning, they might not have reacted with her speed – after all, the Tudor age was one quite accustomed to death – but they, too, would have done exactly what Daphne Pedlinge did and rung for help and told their waiting women that there was a body in the maze and to do something about it.

Miss Pedlinge also pointed out to a shocked Milly that, in the fullness of time, Pete Carter and his brush and shovel would be happening upon it, and that something should be done about that, too.

And quickly.

Chapter Two

Mondays were not usually the busiest day of the week at Berebury Police Station – in theory, that is.

Saturday held the crown in that respect, especially if there happened to be a football match in the town; even more so if the game was a local Derby played between neighbouring teams. Fixtures between, say, Berebury United or Calleford City called for a lot of policing. When the industrial town of Luston played their away match at Berebury, often enough it was extra ambulances that were needed rather than policemen.

On the other hand, Mondays weren't the quietest day of the week at the police station, either.

Not by a long chalk.

As far as Detective Inspector C.D. Sloan was concerned, they didn't have quiet days there at all. And he thought he was a man in a good position to know. After all, he was head of the tiny Criminal Investigation Department of 'F' Division of the County of Calleshire Constabulary. Reports of such crime as there was in that division usually landed on his desk. Detective

Inspector Sloan was known to his nearest and dearest as Christopher Dennis and – for obvious reasons – to his friends and colleagues at the police station as 'Seedy'. His superior officer, however, used neither of these names this morning when he sent for him.

'Ah, there you are, Sloan!' Superintendent Leeyes glared at him from under bushy eyebrows. 'Don't just stand there. Come in. There's been a very odd message from a care assistant to an old lady out in the sticks.' He looked down at a message sheet in his hand. 'Over Staple St James way. At Aumerle Court—'

'The Pedlinges' place,' responded Detective Inspector Sloan, himself a Calleshire man born and bred. He didn't say so, but – as the old phrase had it – the Pedlinge family were 'as well known as the bell man'. 'It's over towards Calleford.'

'The carer – Milly Smithers is her name – says', went on the Superintendent, still staring down at the paper on his desk, 'that her old lady insists there's a dead body in the grounds.'

'And what does the carer say on her own account, sir?' asked Sloan, a man who, in his time had had his full meed of the dotty and the delusional. In the police force, dealing with the mentally deranged had always gone with the territory. Every beat officer got quite good at it early on in his career.

'This Milly Smithers agrees that there's definitely a person lying out there – she could see it, too, from where the old lady is – but she herself isn't absolutely sure that it is a dead one.'

'And what, may I ask, sir,' enquired Sloan, 'makes the old lady think that she knows better?' Their Station Sergeant had daily visits from a man who was unshakeably convinced that his television dish was picking up messages from alien bodies on Mars; messages of an obscure nature that nevertheless the police should do something about then and there. If not sooner.

'She doesn't think,' growled Leeyes. 'She knows . . .'

'Ah.'

'She says it was her wartime service in the FANYs,' quoted Leeyes. He scowled. 'I think someone somewhere must be trying to have us on, Sloan.'

'They may not be, sir.' He frowned. 'I rather think that there was a women's outfit in the Services in the last war known as the FANYs. The First Aid Nursing Yeomanry or something like that. FANYs for short.'

'And there was I', marvelled the Superintendent, 'thinking about Sweet Fanny Adams instead.'

'Yes, sir,' said Sloan stolidly.

'Anyway,' Leeyes snorted, 'the carer wanted to send for an ambulance, but apparently the old lady wouldn't hear of it. Made her carer send for us instead. Insisted on it, in fact.'

'Do we know why, sir?' He had an idea that in their day – in the war, that is – the FANYs had done something clandestine, but he didn't know exactly what.

'She – that's this Miss Daphne Pedlinge—'

'The old lady at Aumerle Court,' put in Sloan,

getting out his notebook. It – a name and address, that is – was as good a place as any to begin.

'She said that the ambulance people might destroy the evidence.'

'So Miss Pedlinge thinks we need to be there first, does she?' mused Sloan. 'That's interesting, sir. And that she thinks there's evidence to be destroyed, too. That's interesting as well.'

The Superintendent wasn't really listening. 'I don't know about getting there first, Sloan, but she says that the police do need to reach the body before a workman called Pete Carter gets to the spot with his shovel and dustbin.' He sniffed. 'What does she imagine he's going to do? Sweep it up and put it on the rubbish tip? Sounds to me as if you'd better take a straitjacket out there with you.'

'Yes, sir.' He sighed unenthusiastically. 'Presumably this Milly Smithers will be able to direct us to the body.'

'I shouldn't count on it if I were you, Sloan.'

'Sir?'

'What you are going to be looking for is lying somewhere in the famous Aumerle maze,' said the Superintendent, adding, quite unabashed, 'Didn't I say?'

'No, sir,' Sloan said expressionlessly. 'You didn't say.'

'Well, it is, and I don't want you and your Sergeant spending all morning playing about in there either.'

'I'm afraid, sir,' said Detective Inspector Sloan with an even more marked lack of enthusiasm, 'that I'll

have to take young Crosby with me today instead.'
Detective Constable Crosby, inexperienced and inept,
was not a useful man to have at his side – or anyone
else's – on a case. 'Sergeant Gelven rang in sick first
thing this morning. He's not going to be well enough to
be on duty at all this week.'

'That's the worst of Monday mornings,' pronounced
Leeyes elliptically. 'They come after Saturday nights.'

But it wasn't the worst of this Monday morning.

By any means.

There was one place in the County of Calleshire where
Monday was definitely not the busiest day of the week
and that was the Bishop's Palace at Calleford.

'Your egg's done, Bertie,' a woman's voice called up
the stairs. 'Don't let it get cold.'

'Coming.' His Grace, the Bishop of Calleford, the
Right Reverend Bertram Wallingford, always made
sure that Monday was kept as a day of rest by the
simple device of remaining in his pyjamas and
dressing gown as long as he could, and staying in bed
as late as his wife would let him.

'I'm putting the toast in now,' said the same voice a
few minutes later, more firmly this time.

'I'm on my way.' A moment later a dishevelled
figure arrived at the table and sat down heavily, fin-
gering an unshaven chin.

Mary Wallingford regarded her husband with
despair. 'It's just as well you've already got preferment

in the Church, Bertie. If anyone in the diocese saw you now they'd say you'd never make a curate, let alone get a bishopric.'

'They would if I were non-stipendiary,' he said realistically. 'In my opinion you can get away with murder in the Church of England if you don't need paying.'

'And,' she said, undeflected, 'if any of the women's groups in Calleshire which I give my talks to ever caught sight of you in that deplorable dressing gown, they'd drum me out immediately.'

Unabashed, the Bishop looked down at what had once been a brown-and-white checked pattern. 'What's wrong with it?'

'Old age,' she said crisply.

'People live longer these days,' he said. 'Why shouldn't dressing gowns?'

'You shall have a new one for Christmas.'

'That sounds more like a threat than a promise.' He gave a great yawn and stretched his arms upwards. 'That was a very good meal last night, Mary. One of your best.'

'You can't beat a good beef casserole,' said the Bishop's wife, well versed in dishes that could wait upon the end of Evensong (with sermon). 'And a plum tart afterwards.'

'It did Malby a power of good, anyway,' said the Bishop, running his hands through his tousled grey hair. 'Poor fellow. He does so look forward to your Sunday evening suppers now.'

'It must be very lonely at the Deanery these days,' said Mary Wallingford. 'Not having a wife to come home to any more . . .'

'And to share your worries with,' finished Bertie Wallingford simply. He had made a practice throughout their marriage of pouring out his own troubles – or nearly all of them – to his wife as soon as he stepped back over his own threshold. He gave this fact, and her, all the credit for his not having succumbed early – like many better men in the Church – to a coronary thrombosis.

'I thought deans didn't have any worries,' she said, tongue-in-cheek, 'and that only bishops and archdeacons did . . . or have I got that wrong?'

'Malby's got worries,' said the Bishop earnestly. 'Big ones.'

'Not the Church Commissioners again, I hope?'

He shook his head. 'There's been a sudden outbreak of prowlers in the Close, for one thing. The security people don't seem able to do anything about them – it's not as if the Minster is enclosed—'

'A precinct would be safer,' she agreed, echoing, had she known it, many an early medieval builder.

'And then . . .'. He paused.

'And then?' she prompted him.

'And then, first thing the other morning one of the gardeners found some odd things outside Canon Willoughby's front door.'

'How odd, exactly, these things?' she queried.

He hesitated. 'If you must know—'

'Of course I must know, Bertie,' Mary Wallingford interrupted him impatiently. 'Don't be silly.'

'What I think you might call signs of uncanonical practices.'

'Such as?'

'A sheep's head.' He dropped his gaze. 'And some burnt feathers and other things.'

'Ah,' she nodded. 'I thought Malby was rather quiet last night.'

'He told me not to worry you.'

'That was nice of him.'

'So', hurried on the Bishop, 'the Chapter has asked that firm in Berebury which has been so efficient with the Minster floodlighting . . .'

'Double Felix, Ltd.' Her lips twitched. 'Such a clever name – and neat, too, having those "two cats rampant" as their logo. That's really brilliant.'

'Them,' said the Bishop, hitting his egg with a spoon. 'Malby told the Clerk of Works to get them in as a matter of urgency. They've been putting up some more security lights in any especially dark corners in the Close.'

'Good,' said Mary. 'You never know what's going to happen next when people start to get funny ideas about the Church.'

'Well, you needn't worry now because Double Felix are working on it flat out. I know that because Malby and I saw their head-wallah – David somebody . . . I forget his name—'

'Collins,' she supplied.

'That's right – him – still at it in the slype yesterday evening when we came across here for supper after the service.'

'I expect David Collins is quite glad to get out of the house just now,' said the Bishop's wife sympathetically. 'Work is a very present help in time of trouble. It can sometimes take your mind off other things.'

'Of course.' The Bishop bowed his head. 'I was forgetting about his little boy's illness. He's not any worse, is he?'

'Not that I've heard,' said his wife, 'but it's a nasty operation for a young child, losing an eye like that, and you never know with that sort of cancer, do you?'

'We've a lot to be thankful for,' he said humbly. 'How do you come to know all this about the Collins family?'

'Margaret – that's his wife – comes in from Nether Hoystings to our pre-school nursery with the boy.' Being the treasurer of this was just one of Mary Wallingford's many voluntary jobs. 'She's quite a striking-looking woman in a rather sultry way, but always very pleasant to talk to. They're both shattered about the eye naturally. He's an only child, too.'

The Bishop nodded. 'I can understand the man throwing himself into his work—'

'Even if it's in the slype after hours on a Sunday?' Mary Wallingford shivered. 'I've never liked the place. Nasty, narrow and dark . . .'

'Well, at least it's not going to be dark for long.'

Bertie Wallingford started to cut his buttered toast into nursery-sized 'soldiers'. 'But I'm afraid', he added drily, 'even the Dean can't do anything about the slype being so narrow – he'd have to move the Chapter House first.'

'And yet, Bertie,' his wife gave him a teasing smile, tongue well in cheek, 'you're always saying that compared with bishops, deans have all the power in the world.'

'And even with Malby Coton's very considerable autonomy, he can't shift the Minster transept either.' The Bishop reached for the salt. 'And as for the slype being nasty . . .'

'Yes?'

'It's not as nasty as having a sheep's head on your doorstep.' He turned his head. 'Is that the doorbell?'

'It'll be the postman.'

'I'll go,' he said.

'Not in that dressing gown, you won't,' said Mary Wallingford vigorously. 'It'll be enough to turn him from Christianity.'

'I expect the man's an agnostic anyway. Nearly everyone seems to be these days.'

'To atheism, then,' she said, rising to her feet. 'I'm going anyway.'

She was back in an instant, her face white, her hand shaking a little. 'Oh, Bertie, do come . . . it was the postman. But there's a dead rabbit lying on the doorstep as well—'

'Dropped by a fox, I expect, my dear,' he said

suppressing another, less welcome thought. 'They're urban creatures these days.'

She shook her head. 'No, no, Bertie, it wasn't a fox. It's got a rusty old wire twisted round its neck, poor thing. Besides, there's a collection of little bones on the path inside some chalk lines.' She gulped. 'And something somewhere's making a very funny noise.'

Chapter Three

Offices are places where Monday mornings are never popular. Almost as soon as she had arrived at work, Sharon Gibbons, secretary to the rising firm of Double Felix Ltd, Lighting Specialists, of Chapel Street, Berebury, brought a load of files into the partners' room and placed them firmly on Eric Paterson's desk.

'Hey, Sharon, steady on,' Paterson protested, flipping open the file on the top of the pile. 'These aren't all mine.'

'I'm sorry, Eric,' apologized David Collins, the other half of Double Felix Ltd, who was sitting at the desk opposite. He grimaced. 'I'm afraid they're mostly mine.'

The two partners could not have been more different. Eric Paterson was an unkempt, shambling figure, never seemingly stressed, while David Collins, his dark-haired, intense partner, was much thinner, more precise and perpetually wound up. The combination of the two opposites worked well and Double Felix Ltd had as much highly specialized lighting work on its hands as it could cope with.

'And it's not Sharon's fault, Eric,' continued David Collins, poised to leave his desk. He gave Sharon a swift glance of sympathy. 'I've got to get off up to the hospital in half a tick. Mr Beaumont, the oncology consultant, wants a word with Margaret and me about little James this morning.'

'It's only routine, though, David, isn't it?' asked his business partner uneasily.

'Just a follow-up, they called it,' responded David Collins, 'although they did keep James in over the weekend. They said not to worry,' he gave a wan smile, 'but I must say that that's always a bit difficult in the circumstances and Margaret gets very wound up.'

'Naturally,' put in Sharon.

'Doctors always say not to worry,' growled the other man, 'even though they know you won't believe them. Not an ounce of imagination, the medical profession. Mind you,' Paterson added, 'I'm sure it's very different when it's one of them who's ill.'

'I daresay you're right,' said David Collins, nodding. 'Actually, Margaret stayed overnight at the hospital with James because he gets quite het up when he has to go back in there—'

'You can't blame him, can you?' interposed Sharon, all motherly sympathy. 'Poor little chap.'

'Anyway, I'll be back as soon as we've seen the oncologist,' said Collins, making for the door. 'It shouldn't take long and then I'll just nip over to the Minster and finish off what I didn't get done last night.'

Sharon Gibbons waited until David Collins had

gone before she said, 'You can tell he was worried really, can't you, Eric? He always tugs at that tall tuft of hair that sticks up over his forehead when he's got something on his mind. I've noticed.'

'Does he?' said Eric Paterson, his mind elsewhere. His own hair was always all over the place, though he doubted if their secretary ever noticed that.

'Sorry, Eric, all the same, about giving you all the files,' Sharon said unrepentantly, waving a hand at the pile of them she'd put on his desk.

'I'm sure,' grunted the partner, knowing what she said to be untrue.

'I'm afraid you'll have to take a look at them this morning . . .' Sharon Gibbons had never doubted that Monday was the most difficult day of the week and there was nothing on the agenda for today likely to make her change her mind. '. . . we'd better be on the safe side.'

Eric Paterson grunted again and picked up the next file down the heap.

Experienced secretary that she was, Sharon kept silent. She knew only too well that tensions left unresolved on Friday afternoons could ripen into open warfare by Monday morning. Not that Eric Paterson went in for tension much. Not him.

He picked up the third file.

Sharon also knew that problems which have lain untouched in in-trays all weekend have not thus mysteriously solved themselves: and that they tend, instead, to rise up again even as the worker, not helped by a weekend of brooding on the subject, pulls up the chair to the desk. The members of the firm of Double Felix Ltd were no exception to this general rule and Sharon Gibbons was busy.

'But these are all David's files,' insisted Eric Paterson, looking up from the next one down the stack. 'Every one of them.'

'David, if you remember,' Sharon said, unmoved, 'went over to Aumerle Court yesterday afternoon to look at the maze and was working until late last night over at Calleford Minster, quite apart from having to go off to the hospital this morning.'

'So he was,' Eric admitted easily. 'I'd forgotten how determined he was to get on with that church job this weekend. He's a better man than I am, I must say,' he added, knowing that Sharon would have a hard job not agreeing with him aloud.

'That's David for you all over,' said Sharon tactfully. She much preferred David Collins, the younger, more active partner, and his pale determined look. 'He said to me that he was keen to get the Minster work over and done with as soon as he could so that he could get cracking on some other jobs that have been piling up.'

'Which they have,' he reminded her, 'in quite a big way.'

'Have a heart, Eric,' she said. 'You can't expect David to concentrate on his work while his son's been so ill. It wouldn't be natural.'

'Work's work,' said her employer implacably.

'I know, I know,' she sighed, 'and it's all got to be done somehow.'

'And you can give him this file straight away when he does get back,' said David's partner, tossing a thick green bundle over on to the other desk. 'It's the Aumerle Court project, Heaven help us all. Thank God it's one of his.'

'I don't know', Sharon went on as if he hadn't spoken, 'how nearly David finished the Minster job yesterday evening. But the Clerk of Works has been on the phone already this morning. They want him back there, very pronto, like always.'

'You'd better tell David as soon as he comes in, then,' Paterson grinned, adding, 'and they'll both have to wait anyway until he does come back to the office since mobile phones aren't allowed at either the Minster or the hospital. Not quite the forces of God and Mammon, but nearly.' He twirled his pencil. 'Perhaps we should say God and the hospital. Comes to same thing, doesn't it? The doctors over there all think they're God—'

'It's their Canon Willoughby at the Minster,' she interrupted him. 'He wants some extra security lighting installed outside his house in the Close, now, if not sooner.'

Eric Paterson scratched his chin. 'More trouble there?'

'Something cabbalistic written in charcoal on his doorstep is what they told us,' said Sharon. 'I'm not sure if the old boy knows what it means—'

'But if he does, he's not saying,' finished Paterson for her.

'But whatever it is, they don't like it there in the Close.'

'There's a lot of things they don't like in the Close,' said Eric Paterson, absently leafing through the file. 'Hey, Sharon, you're slipping. This next letter here is in the wrong place.'

Sharon Gibbons stiffened. 'What letter? Where? Show me.'

'This one. Here, in the Minster file.' Paterson was regarding it with fine detachment. 'About circuits.'

'Well, I don't know how that got in there, I'm sure,' she said defensively. 'That's not the Aumerle Court file.'

'No, it's the Minster one, as I said, but here's a rough plan of Aumerle Court and another stroppy diatribe from that toy soldier over at Staple St James—'

'Captain Prosser,' said Sharon, identifying the gentleman in question without difficulty like the good secretary she was. She sniffed. 'I don't know when the Captain thinks David is going to get over to Aumerle Court while he's as busy as he is.'

'Yesterday, from the tone of his letter,' said Paterson, quite relaxed, 'if not the day before. Ring him – no, write, that'll take longer to get there, which will annoy him – and tell him that we'll come when we can and not a minute before. I don't like Double Felix being leaned on by the likes of him.'

'Their *son-et-lumière* performances are due to be put on quite soon,' murmured Sharon with apparent disinterest. 'The end of the month, I think it's supposed to be. David was saying that the actual date's something to do with when it's going to be dark enough in the evening, which', she added obliquely, 'it will be before long. He was trying to find time to get over there.'

'Oh, all right, then,' Paterson said, still unperturbed. 'Put this one on David's desk and I'll talk to him about it as soon as I set eyes on him.' He locked his fingers behind his head and leaned back lazily in his swivel chair. 'The rest of all this paperwork you can take away and go through while I sit and think about object waves meeting reference waves and cabbages and kings.'

Sharon Gibbons said nothing, but she could not resist a reproving glance at the clock.

'Unless you'd like to bring me some coffee instead,' he said, seeing this and grinning. 'After all, one of us has to have our work priorities right.'

Reaching the entrance of the maze at Aumerle Court presented Detective Inspector Sloan and Detective Constable Crosby with no problems at all. It was a simple matter of driving out of the market town of Berebury towards Calleford and making their way through the Calleshire countryside to the little village of Staple St James.

Getting inside the labyrinth itself proved quite a different matter. Blocking the way in with a large green dustbin on wheels was Kenny Prickett. A foot soldier manqué, he was mounting guard against all-comers, holding his broom with the bristles aloft with one hand and looking for all the world like a latterday Britannia complete with trident. His other hand clutched his shovel – in his mind's eye already an entrenching tool – very much at the ready.

'Miss Daphne sent a message to say I wasn't to let no one in', he said firmly, 'until the police came.'

Detective Inspector Sloan nodded. 'Quite right,' he murmured abstractedly, surveying the vast area of impenetrable yew hedge on either side of the narrow entrance.

'And to listen hard in case Pete called out.' Kenny Prickett relaxed a little and lowered his broom to a sort of stand-easy position.

'And has he?' enquired Sloan.

'Not yet,' said Kenny. 'Miss Daphne said he would, but not for a bit. Haven't heard a dicky bird from him yet, but I will. Bound to when he gets to this body that Miss Daphne says is in there.' Like Milly Smithers, Kenny Prickett had been born in Staple St James and took Daphne Pedlinge's word for law. 'Pete's never liked being in the maze. Not ever.' He jerked his shoulder upwards in the direction of the house. 'Miss Daphne said Pete wouldn't have got to Ariadne yet, let alone any further in.'

'Who's Ariadne?' asked Detective Constable Crosby, bringing up the rear and taking out his own notebook at the mention of a name.

'A statue,' responded Kenny.

The Constable looked disappointed.

'It's a lady with a ball of wool, that's all,' explained Kenny, parking his broom against the yew hedge.

'How do you mean "all"?' demanded Crosby, his pen hovering unused above his notebook.

'I mean that's all she's got on,' said Kenny Prickett simply.

'A ball of wool?' echoed Crosby, disbelievingly.

'Miss Daphne said that Ariadne had something to do with mazes in history,' explained the man, 'and the ball of wool was what she gave to her lover to help him get in and out of the maze.'

'Get away,' said Crosby.

'She did. Tied it to the entrance and told him not to let it go so that he could find his way out again. That's why she's in there.'

'Is there a plan of the maze?' asked Sloan briskly. Tempting as it was to send his Detective Constable into the maze then and there without one, it probably wouldn't help the investigation in the long run. In the end someone was bound to have to go in and find him again.

Kenny Prickett scratched his head. 'They say that Miss Daphne's got one in her room but no one's ever seen it. Take all the fun away, wouldn't it, if everyone had the plan?'

'Very probably,' said Sloan wryly. He didn't see any point in solving puzzles purely for pleasure, but then he was a working policeman. He had to solve puzzles anyway – without maps – most of the time; and without any pleasure all of the time.

'I can tell you that Ariadne's about halfway in,' volunteered Kenny Prickett. He stood down his shovel, too, propping it up against the yew hedge. 'There's a seat by her, and Pete usually stops there, Mondays, for a bit of a breather after he's done her alcove. Not too long, of course,' he added, 'on account of Miss Daphne watching and the Captain waiting.'

'Ah . . .' said Detective Inspector Sloan alertly. He spun round on his heel and looked behind him. Soaring upwards was the elegant diapered brickwork of the eastern wall of a fine Elizabethan house. At first-floor level, and overlooking this part of the grounds, was a mullioned window. It was impossible to tell at this distance whether or not anyone was looking out of it.

'It usually takes either of us the best part of an hour to work our way round to Ariadne,' offered Kenny, 'give or take a load of extra rubbish to clear up. Broken glass can make you very late.'

Sloan nodded. He'd never yet met an occupation without hazards. It seemed that broken glass was one that dustmen shared with policemen.

'You'd be surprised what people leave in there,' Kenny sniffed. 'And you never know what some people'll get up to Sunday afternoons when they haven't got anything better to do.'

'We do know,' interposed Detective Constable Crosby feelingly. 'A day with the family brings out the worst in some.'

'Are you going to go in, then?' asked Kenny directly.

'Would we be able to find the statue in there if we did?' countered Crosby.

'Doubt it,' said Kenny laconically. He pulled his dustcart away from the entrance to the maze and waved a hand. 'Be my guest. Mind you, Ariadne's up one of the blind alleys so you might get there by accident. A lot of people do.'

'Couldn't you just take us straight there?' suggested Crosby, staring beyond the little ticket booth just inside the entrance. The path ahead gave way to a narrow walkway between two high hedges, which was singularly without signposts of any sort.

'Not me,' said Kenny. 'Besides, Miss Daphne said I wasn't to go in.'

'Quite,' said Sloan. The man was clearly good military material in the matter of always obeying the last order.

'Told me to send you straight up to the house when you arrived, she did. Said it was a waste of time for you to go inside the maze on your own and she should know . . . Hello,' he jerked his head back, 'here comes trouble.'

Sloan followed the direction of his gaze as another figure appeared on the scene. He was dressed in a lightly checked soft shirt, regimental tie and a tweed hacking jacket.

'Captain Jeremy Prosser,' the man said, advancing on them in highly polished brogues, a clipboard tucked under one arm. 'I'm the steward here.'

'Police,' said Detective Inspector Sloan, without explanation. The newcomer might just as well have been in uniform. Sloan wasn't.

'I've just heard there's a problem with the maze,' said Jeremy Prosser.

'In the maze,' Kenny Prickett corrected him swiftly. 'There's nothing wrong with the maze, Captain.'

'Pete Carter should be in there now, clearing up,' Prosser said to the two policemen, ignoring this. 'If he's up to schedule, that is.'

'Pete is in there,' said Kenny briefly.

'Unless he came out before we got here,' contributed Detective Constable Crosby helpfully.

'Miss Daphne says he's in the maze,' said Kenny, as one citing the laws of the Medes and the Persians.

'And she should know,' put in Jeremy Prosser smoothly. 'She has the best view of us all.'

'No one,' said Detective Inspector Sloan baldly, 'is going in or out of there until I say so.'

The effect of this grand pronouncement was undermined almost immediately as a great shout reached them from inside the maze.

'See? I told you that Pete was still in there, didn't I?' remarked Kenny with satisfaction. He threw his head back and hollered, 'Where are you, mate?'

'Here,' came a muffled voice from somewhere within. 'Can you come and get me, Kenny? There's something here that shouldn't be.'

'Whereabouts exactly?' called out Jeremy Prosser.

'In the middle,' came the voice, a certain truculence

creeping into its tone in response to the steward. 'By the bull. The one they call the Minotaur.'

'Police here,' said Sloan crisply. 'What exactly have you found?'

'A woman,' came the distant reply. 'She's dead . . .' The rest of the sentence was lost as a cock blackbird, alarmed by something, fluttered upwards, squawking.

'Come again?' shouted Kenny to Pete.

'Dead,' came the voice through the yew. 'Really dead.'

Chapter Four

David Collins pushed open the double doors to the children's ward at the Berebury and District General Hospital with just the right amount of pressure. He'd been through them so many times now that he could gauge exactly how much shove with a straight arm they took to shift.

'Ah, Mr Collins, there you are.' The Ward Sister greeted him as he stepped on to the ward. All the nurses knew him by name now, he'd visited his son so often. 'We wondered when you'd be along. James has had a good night and he's all ready to see Mr Beaumont when he does his ward round.'

'Good,' said David Collins.

'After that', she smiled, taking in with a swift professional glance his tired face and the controlled anxiety she saw in so many of the parents of her patients, 'I'm sure you're going to be able to take him home with you today.'

'Until next time,' he said soberly.

'He's going to need monitoring for quite a while yet,' the Sister said seriously. 'It wouldn't be right for us not to continue with our usual follow-up.'

'I know, I know,' he said wearily. 'But we – my wife and I – get the feeling that we'll never be finished with hospitals.' He opened his hands in a gesture of despair. 'I'm sorry, but you know how it is.'

'We understand all that,' she said, still serious. 'And we all know how trying your wife finds it. It's never easy, living with a child with this sort of condition.'

'Did Margaret get any sleep at all last night?' he asked. 'She said she'd try to as soon as James dropped off.'

'Last night?' echoed the Sister. 'I don't know whether she did last night – she wasn't here. At least,' she frowned, 'I don't think she was. I wasn't on duty myself but there was nothing in the morning report about her being here overnight.'

'She was,' he said, unruffled. 'I brought her in quite early in the afternoon and she was going to stay on here with James. Poor little chap doesn't like hospitals, and anyway Mr Beaumont wanted to see us both together this morning. As I was going to work late yesterday evening it seemed the simplest thing to do.'

'I certainly haven't seen her around today myself.' The Ward Sister looked across the ward. 'Dr Chomel over there may know because she was on duty yesterday as well as this morning.'

David Collins looked puzzled. 'I was expecting my wife to be here to see Mr Beaumont with me as we arranged—'

'You ask Dr Chomel,' advised the Sister, 'and I'll be with you as soon as Mr Beaumont arrives.'

Dr Dilys Chomel was leaning over James Collins's hospital cot making a paper airplane for him. 'Now, you throw it, James . . . no, aim for me. That's a clever boy.' She straightened up as David approached. 'Now, James, look who's come to see you.'

'Daddy,' said James, only looking up cursorily from his paper toy before throwing it at Dr Chomel again.

'Isn't it nice to see him?' said the young doctor, neatly fielding the paper dart and explaining that she was using it to test James's co-ordination and aim now that he only had one eye.

'Mummy,' said the little boy. 'I want my mummy.'

'I expect she's come too,' said Dr Chomel brightly, looking round.

'She hasn't,' said David Collins. 'Actually, I thought she'd been here overnight with James. That's what we had arranged. She's stayed in your parents' room often enough before now.'

'I want my mummy,' said James again.

'No.' Dr Chomel shook her head and moved out of earshot of the child. 'Mrs Collins was here in the afternoon because I saw her and we talked about James and how soon he could have his artificial eye fitted—'

'I know she's been worrying a lot about that,' David Collins volunteered.

'She was a bit upset about it, naturally, but I hope I was able to reassure her,' said the House Surgeon, beginning to sound quite anxious herself. 'Children of this age take something like artifical eyes on board so much more easily than grown-ups do.' She forbore to explain that in the African country from which she came the loss of an eye was common and that it was the artificial replacement that was the rarity.

'That's what everyone's always telling us, but it wasn't that.' David Collins grimaced. 'It was the thought of having to see the empty socket that really got to Margaret.'

'I don't think Mr Beaumont will want James's bandages left off just yet,' the doctor murmured obliquely.

'But it's going to happen one day,' he said, 'and Margaret just doesn't want to be around when it does. She keeps on saying so.'

'I want my mummy,' declared James Collins even more insistently.

'All right, James,' said Dr Chomel, going back over to him. 'Daddy and I'll go and find Mummy for you now. You look after your airplane until I get back.'

Her manner changed as soon as she was alone with David Collins. 'Mr Collins, are you telling me that your wife didn't come home last night?'

'I am,' he said flatly. 'That's what's worrying me. You know how much this terrible illness of James's has upset her – both of us, actually.' He frowned. 'I don't think she would have gone over to her mother's without saying. But I suppose she just might have done.'

'Of course,' said the doctor, 'but even so—'

'And she's not been sleeping either what with all the anxiety of the operation and knowing James had to have his eye out.' He clenched his fists tightly. 'It's not fair on a child,' he said in anguished tones. 'He's scarcely more than a baby.'

'It's very hard on everybody,' said the doctor earnestly. 'I was as reassuring with her as I could be yesterday – I do hope, though, that I didn't upset her too much, talking about the new eye.'

David Collins essayed a small smile. 'I am personally quite sure, Doctor, that in no time at all James will be charging his little mates at school for taking it out and letting them look at it. But you'll understand that Margaret can't quite see it like that just yet.'

'It's early days,' she said, looking at him with concern. 'James really is doing well, you know.'

'Well?' he echoed, putting his hand to his head.

'Really well,' she insisted.

'As well as can be expected,' he said ironically. 'That's what they all say here, isn't it? Always.'

'You and your wife must believe me. Please find her and tell her that.'

'But', he opened his hands in a frantic gesture 'where is she?'

The House Surgeon didn't answer him. She had turned her head in response to a sudden stirring of activity at the ward doors. 'I'm sorry, Mr Collins. I must go now. Mr Beaumont has arrived to do his ward round.'

* * * * *

Deplorable old dressing gown or not, Bertram Wallingford stood on the threshold for a long moment and
then slowly advanced towards the dead rabbit.

'Mind where you tread, Bertie,' adjured his wife
anxiously. 'I'm sure those chalk lines mean something.'

'They're a pentagram,' said the Bishop, stepping
carefully round the rabbit laid out on the doorstep to
take a better look at the lines of black chalk round the
bones, which had been set in a rough circle.

'But what does it all mean?' asked Mary.

'The pentagram's a magic symbol—'

'Black magic?'

The Bishop stood back. 'Magic which supposedly
invokes the power of the devil to perform evil.'

'In the Minster Close at Calleford?' she protested.
'Surely not here of all places?'

'I don't think there's anywhere off-limits to the
devil,' said the Bishop quite seriously, 'any more than
there is to Christ. It wouldn't be logical.' He peered
down at the dead rabbit. 'You're quite right, my dear.
We can't blame Monsieur Reynard for this.'

'No,' said Mary Wallingford tightly.

'Nor a cunning little vixen,' he murmured. 'At
least, I don't think so,' he added, half under his
breath. In the nature of things, there were some
women in every congregation of whom all clerics had
to be wary.

'Foxes can't tie wire round the necks of rabbits,'
said his wife.

'And they can't draw diagrams either, can they?' said her husband, staring at the chalked lines.

Margaret Wallingford's head came up suddenly. 'What was that?'

'What was what?'

'That sound.'

'I didn't hear anything.'

'I could have sworn I heard that noise again.'

'What sort of noise?'

'Oh, I don't know – an animal noise. I'm pretty sure it's coming from the West Canonry.'

'The Shorthouses' dogs are in kennels while they're away, so it can't be them,' said Bertram Wallingford.

'Not a bark,' she said. 'More of a bleat.'

He lifted his head and began to say that he couldn't hear anything when the great bell of the Minster began to sound the hour and nobody in the Close could hear anything else at all until it had done.

'Bertie,' Mary Wallingford said shakily, 'does this mean that someone wishes you harm?'

'It might.' He paused and thought for a moment before he said, 'And perhaps not only me.'

Mary Wallingford shivered. 'Me, too, you mean? But why?' She stopped, remembering something. 'So this is what has been worrying Malby—'

'The same thing happened to Canon Willoughby the other day,' admitted Bertie.

'I see.' She gave a mirthless little laugh. 'Isn't it awful how it takes your own troubles to bring home somebody else's?'

'It is, my dear.' He tapped their doorstep with his foot. 'Which, when you come to think about it, is yet another case of sermons in stones.'

'Bertie, I'd have gone round and seen him if I'd heard about what had been left outside the Canonry,' she said, stricken with remorse. 'Why didn't you tell me?'

'I did go round,' said her husband. 'He's taken it in his stride. Apparently, years ago, when he was a curate in Luston he caught some people saying a black mass in his churchyard. They were using a table grave for an altar.'

'What did he do?'

'Gave them black eyes, I think. Brian believed in the church militant in those days. He was young then, of course, and fitter.'

'Bertie,' she interrupted him urgently. 'What about Malby? Have these people been doing nasty things like this at the Deanery, too?'

'They haven't to date, my dear, though I don't know yet about last night. I think our security people ought to know about this first. I'll go indoors now and ring them,' he said, 'and then I'll slip straight over to the Deanery and find out if Malby's had any trouble—'

'Not until you're properly dressed, you won't,' said his wife immediately. 'What would people say?'

Chapter Five

Eric Paterson was still leaning back in his chair when Sharon Gibbons brought him in his mug of coffee. He had his eyes closed, a tacitly agreed sign in the office that he was thinking deeply about a technical problem and did not want to be interrupted by anyone.

This time, though, she didn't leave his mug noiselessly on his desk. Breaking unwritten convention, she plonked the coffee mug down on the desk very firmly and said, 'Eric . . .'

'What is it?' he asked, elaborately patient.

'This matters, Eric . . .'

He opened his eyes and, without looking at her, transferred his gaze to the ceiling, anxious not to lose his train of thought.

'I've just had David on the phone from the hospital—'

That brought his head down and his eyes into focus quickly enough. 'James isn't worse?'

'No,' she frowned. 'It's not James. He seems to be all right. No, it's Margaret.'

'What about her?'

'She's not there.' Automatically, she pushed the sugar towards Eric, although this time without her customary gesture of disapproval. 'Or, rather, she's not been seen at the hospital since yesterday afternoon. That's when David took her over there before he went on to Aumerle Court and the Minster at Calleford.'

Eric Paterson sat up straight. 'What do you mean?'

'Well, David thought she'd been at the hospital with James all night, like he said to us this morning. She often does stay, you know. The nurses like it when a parent is there on the ward.'

'Saves them work,' said Eric, reaching for the sugar.

'The children like it, too,' said Sharon in chilly tones.

'And she hasn't been there?' Eric helped himself to two large teaspoonsful of sugar. 'That's odd.'

'Not since the little lamb went off to sleep during the afternoon. Apparently Margaret told the Staff Nurse that she would slip away and be back again in the morning.'

'And she wasn't,' concluded Eric, reaching for another spoonful of sugar.

'No. She isn't on the ward or at home,' said Sharon, before adding uncertainly, 'She's been under tremendous strain lately, of course.'

'They both have,' said Eric. 'For a long time.'

'Too long.'

'Much too long,' he agreed heavily.

'And they're not out of the woods yet either,' said Sharon compassionately. 'Eric, you don't think—'

Instantly a steely expression settled on his face. 'I never theorize ahead of data, Sharon. It's a great mistake. You should know that. Now, what's David doing about it?'

'They've paged Margaret at the hospital. He rang here just to see if there'd been a message from her – which there hasn't – and then he was going to ring the police.'

'We're sure to find Miss Pedlinge in the Long Gallery, Inspector,' said Jeremy Prosser, leading the way inside Aumerle Court. 'Through here and up these stairs and then along the passage. I'm sure it's the quickest way. . .'

'Good,' said Sloan tersely. He'd left Crosby guarding the entrance to the maze, with strict instructions to keep Kenny Prickett from plunging in and finding his way to Pete Carter's side and the body of an unknown woman.

'I think you'll see that Miss Pedlinge has a bird's eye view of the maze, all right,' said the steward.

'Good,' said Sloan again. He'd told Crosby to make a note of everything that Pete and Kenny said, but he wasn't counting on it being done.

'May we come in?' said the steward, tapping on an ancient oak door on the first-floor landing.

'Do,' called out a sprightly voice.

'This is Detective Inspector Sloan,' announced Prosser.

A wheelchair spun round on oiled wheels and was manoeuvred to face them. 'Ah, the police and the Army . . .'

Sloan was aware of a pair of bright, enquiring eyes looking up at him.

'Two Services must be better than one,' said the old lady in the wheelchair.

'I hope so, madam,' said Detective Inspector Sloan. For all that they were both forces of the Crown, the police always tried to keep their distance from the Army when it came to civil action. But this was not the moment to say so.

'They always used to be when I was a gel.' The old lady's lips twitched enigmatically.

'Quite so,' said Detective Inspector Sloan. 'Now, I understand, madam, that you keep an eye on the grounds from here—'

'Indeed I do.'

'And the maze.'

'Naturally,' she said. 'It's not as old as the one at Hampton Court, but it's getting on.'

Getting on was what Sloan wanted to do more than anything, but he held his peace. He'd discovered long ago that hurrying the old got you nowhere. On the contrary . . .

'I was just watching to see that my Cerberus was doing his guard job properly. Kenny's a good worker – he won't let anyone into the maze if he's been told not to. You can count on it.'

'Carter's found a body—' began Prosser, who could

never bring himself to call the workmen by their Christian names in case they called him by his.

'I know that,' said the old lady impatiently. 'I saw him reach it five minutes ago. It was what I was hoping to stop – I told Milly to tell the police that,' she gave Sloan a baleful look, 'but you didn't get here in time.'

'No,' agreed Detective Inspector Sloan, stepping swiftly towards the window. Without waiting for an answer, he said, 'May I take a look?'

The great hedge maze lay below him, every twist and turn clearly visible from where he was standing. Sloan could make out the figure of a man near the middle of the further right-hand quadrant of the square. The man, whom he supposed to be Pete Carter, was standing beside a body which was only partly visible to Sloan from where he was standing on the first floor.

It was lying, apparently face downwards, in a little clear space in front of a statue. Pete Carter – if, indeed, it was he who was beside the body – was trying to hold up a broom above the surrounding hedge to indicate where in the maze he was. Even at this distance, Sloan could see, too, that the fellow was still shouting to his mate, Kenny Prickett.

'Where have my binoculars got to now, Milly?' asked Miss Pedlinge, fumbling about behind her with her hand. 'We need them again.'

Milly Smithers pointed. 'They're hanging from the back of your chair, Miss Daphne, like always.'

'Allow me,' murmured Detective Inspector Sloan

ambiguously, lifting the binoculars off their resting place and first raising them to his own eyes. A quick twist of their knurled focus knob brought the scene more clearly into his view. 'Ah, I see . . .'

The body appeared from the clothing to be female, but a stretch of hedge in front of it hid the whole corpse from his view. At this distance it was impossible for Sloan to hazard a guess at the age of whoever was lying there, but there was something indefinable about the way in which it was lying that betokened death as opposed to unconsciousness to him, just as it had done to Miss Pedlinge.

Exactly as vultures are said to be able to determine the precise moment that the life of their prey becomes extinct, so Detective Inspector Sloan could also see what there had been about this figure that had made the old lady so sure they were dealing with more than a simple attack of syncope.

'We need to get into the maze and fast,' he announced crisply, lowering the binoculars.

'Easier said than done, Inspector,' said Jeremy Prosser. 'It's not a unicursal one, you know, in spite of what the men say.'

'Really, sir?' said Sloan distantly. He had a rooted aversion to the use by other people of words they presumed he would not know and understand: the more especially, he was honest enough to admit, when he didn't. Unicursal being one such word.

'And it's no good just putting your right hand on the hedge and keeping going like you can with some mazes,' finished the agent. 'That won't get you any-where.'

'Or your left hand,' remarked Miss Pedlinge. 'That wouldn't be any good, either.'

'What about those two workers?' asked Sloan. 'They must go in there often enough.'

Prosser gave a mirthless laugh. 'They insist that they get lost every time they go in the maze. If you ask me, Inspector, I think it's their way of taking more time on the job.'

'If,' said Detective Inspector Sloan, anxious to get on with his own work and, unlike the two men in question, having no reason to prolong it, 'I were to stay here and guide my Constable in by radio phone, could I direct him to the right spot?'

'No,' said Daphne Pedlinge promptly, 'but I could.'

'Now, Miss Daphne, dear,' protested Milly Smithers, 'you shouldn't be letting yourself get all excited.'

'Rubbish,' said Miss Pedlinge spiritedly. She gave Sloan a wicked grin. 'Beats a visit from the doctor any day.'

Sloan took out his two-way radio and started to call up Detective Constable Crosby. 'Miss Pedlinge, would you say it's the statue of Ariadne that Pete Carter has just passed?'

'No,' said the old lady, 'I wouldn't, even though mazes do have their beginnings in antiquity and she comes into the legend.'

'Ah . . .'

'It would seem, Inspector,' she said astringently,

'that it isn't only your classical education that has been neglected.'

'Madam?' Out of the corner of his eye, Sloan could see Jeremy Prosser quietly picking up the binoculars and pointing them in the direction of the maze.

'That, Inspector,' she said, 'is Theseus, who, as you ought to be able to see even at this distance, is no lady.'

'Quite so, madam.' Sloan realized that Jeremy Prosser's vision through the binoculars by now must have focused on Pete Carter and the body. 'I believe your workman is quite near the middle of the maze, isn't he?'

'It's the centre of the maze that matters, you know,' said Daphne Pedlinge. 'Not the section by Theseus. He went to Crete as one of the seven maidens and seven youths to be sacrificed to the Minotaur and fell in love with Ariadne. She told him the legend of the labyrinth.'

'How to get out?'

'Yes. After he'd killed the Minotaur. Not that it did Ariadne any good. He ditched her afterwards.' Her gaze travelled impartially over policeman and soldier. 'Some men are like that.'

'In what way does the centre of the maze matter?' asked Sloan, subconsciously aware of the blood slowly draining from the cheeks of Captain Prosser.

'You must understand, Inspector,' explained the woman in the wheelchair, 'that the maze is meant to be an allegory of life.'

'Tell me more, madam,' he said, one eye still on Prosser. The man had lowered the binoculars now and was running his tongue over dry lips.

49

'And reaching the centre of the maze, Inspector, is an allegory for death, which it was in fact for the seven maidens and seven youths sacrificed each year to the bull of Minos.' She twisted her lips into a wry smile. 'The end of the quest, don't you know?'

All Detective Inspector Sloan actually knew was that, as Captain Prosser had viewed the body in the maze, a little line of sweat had appeared where his short-back-and-sides hairline met a brow still unaccountably pale, and the hands that handed back the pair of binoculars were now visibly unsteady.

Chapter Six

'Which way next did you say, madam?' asked Detective Inspector Sloan over the radio telephone. He hadn't realized quite how disorientating he would find two tall hedges of yew once he was standing between them, unable to see anything except sky.

'Turn right now and then left as soon as you can,' crackled a distant voice.

In the end, Sloan had gone back to the maze himself and he was now taking instructions at long distance on how to reach the body. They came from the old lady sitting in the Long Gallery at her vantage point well above and behind him. He'd left her his own two-way radio and collected Crosby's from him. The fact that his Detective Constable was now plunging noisily along behind him down the narrow green passages of verdure was a distraction rather than any great help. Kenny Prickett they had left still guarding the entrance, this time with the assistance of Captain Prosser.

'I said left next,' came a peremptory voice over the ether, 'not right.'

'So you did, madam,' he assented. His concentration had slipped while he was making a mental note at the back of his mind about the gallant Captain. As well as demonstrating a sudden pallor and a little burst of perspiration about the hairline when looking through the binoculars, he had shown no great willingness to come as far as the maze, let alone venture inside it. 'My fault.'

'Now left again,' the commanding elderly voice came clearly over the ether.

There were, Sloan realized now, no points of reference inside a maze. The two policemen would have been lost in minutes had not Miss Pedlinge been telling them where to go next.

'And again,' she said.

'If we go on like this, sir,' muttered Crosby mutinously, 'any minute now we'll be back where we started.'

'Now turn right,' came the voice upon the instant, demolishing any theories anyone might have heard about always keeping to the left.

'Ah,' said Sloan. Suddenly the path in front of them splayed out into a circle of yew hedge. In the middle of this was a statue of a woman. 'Would this be Ariadne, I wonder?' he murmured aloud.

Detective Constable Crosby shook his head. 'No, sir,' he said confidently. 'There's no sign that this young lady here's wearing a ball of wool.' He took another look and blinked. 'Or anything else, come to that.'

'Ah,' said the disembodied voice. 'I see you've got to Pasiphaë at last. You're getting warmer . . .'

'Which is more than can be said for her over there,' said Crosby sotto voce, pointing to the statue. 'If she's not frozen stiff, then she ought to be. Not a stitch on.'

'Pasiphaë was the daughter of the sun god Helios,' the two policemen were informed by the old lady inside Aumerle Court.

'Then you'd think she'd feel the cold all the more, wouldn't you, sir?' said Crosby insouciantly. 'So why have they got her in here without anything on?'

'Artistic licence,' said Sloan briefly. He made another mental note. As far as he could tell, neither Miss Daphne Pedlinge, nor her carer, Milly Smithers, had recognized the body, the first sight of whose clothing had brought Captain Prosser out in such a cold sweat. He could, he realized, be wrong about this: the old lady had been cool and collected enough – to say nothing of experienced – to have concealed the fact. 'Keep moving, Crosby.'

'Pasiphaë was the wife of Minos,' went on the scholarly voice of Miss Daphne Pedlinge. 'In the first instance, that is. The bull came later—'

'What bull?' asked Crosby.

'And she was also the mother of Androgeos,' Miss Pedlinge continued. 'His statue is the one you should come to next, gentlemen. Take the further path after the next turning—'

'Can't wait,' said Crosby.

'You'll have to,' said Sloan grimly, 'if you don't listen and pay attention to the lady's instructions.' He led the way forward. 'Follow me—'

'And now turn sharp right,' came the voice through the radio telephone.

'This way,' intruded another sound, this from much nearer and much louder. 'I'm over here,' carried on a man's voice plaintively. 'Pete Carter. With a dead woman. Can't you get to me any quicker, whoever you are?'

'Police,' said Detective Constable Crosby. 'That's who we are and we're coming.'

'Then take the second left,' ordered Miss Pedlinge, 'that should bring you straight to Androgeos.'

'There he is,' said Crosby as they turned left into another round space in the maze. He inspected a conspicuously male statue. 'All boy, isn't he?'

'So I should hope,' said Sloan, 'with a name like that.'

'What?' The Constable looked puzzled and then his face cleared. 'Oh, I get you, sir.' Crosby grinned. 'So that's where the word "androgen" comes from, is it?' He took a longer, more considering look at the statue. 'Well, I never . . .'

'Androgeos', they were told in uninflected tones from the upper room at Aumerle Court, 'beat all-comers in the games at Athens.'

'I can believe that,' said Crosby, brightening. 'Fine-looking fellow, isn't he?'

'So they killed him,' said Miss Pedlinge.

'For winning?' said Crosby. The Berebury football team were always celebrated for their victories. With a vengeance. 'That's pretty dire.'

'Do come,' pleaded an unhappy voice from behind a nearby hedge. 'I don't like it here.'

'You're nearly at the centre of the maze now, Inspector,' said the voice from the window. 'Keep going.'

'Puts a whole new light on those Berebury versus Luston football matches, doesn't it, sir?' said Detective Constable Crosby, demonstrating how a classical education could broaden the mind. 'Being killed for winning, I mean.'

'Losers like the last word,' said Sloan briefly. 'Come on, we must be nearly there.'

'Just one more turning,' said the old lady.

'Here,' called out Pete Carter, 'I'm over here. Can't anyone hear me and come?'

Sloan plunged ahead, taking the last twist in the path at speed.

The two policemen reached the centre of the maze with disconcerting suddenness. The statue there was neither human nor animal but a strange amalgam of both – half bull, half man.

'You've got to the Minotaur now,' said the detached voice over the airwaves. 'The Minotaur, you will remember, was the legendary outcome of a liaison between Pasiphaë and a bull.'

But Detective Inspector Sloan wasn't taking in Greek legends. He was trying to listen to the agitated observations of Pete Carter while at the same time looking down at the dead body of a woman. It was lying at the feet of the Minotaur.

The educated elderly female voice had not finished its spiel. 'And, gentlemen, as I said before, arriving at the figure of the Minotaur traditionally represents the end of man's quest to the centre of the labyrinth, which is, of course, a metaphor for death . . .'

'I'm very sorry, Mr Dean,' Barry Wright was saying. His official title was Clerk of Works at the Minster in Calleford, although he would have much preferred to be known as a manager of some kind. Other people knew what managers were and did: they managed. Nobody knew precisely what lay within the responsibilities of the Clerk of Works; except those living in and around the Minster Close.

There, of course, was the rub.

Barry Wright's early attempts to get his job title modernized had foundered on such intangibles as the Minster Statutes, various early Cathedral Measures Acts and a multitude of precedents established by decisions taken by the Greater Chapter over the last millennium.

His own later attempts to have his duties and responsibilities defined more exactly had had a simpler outcome: in essence they comprised doing whatever the Dean wanted him to do. And sooner rather than later.

He was standing outside the Deanery now with the Dean, the Very Reverend Malby Coton, and the Bishop of Calleford. They were all looking down at a bizarre assortment of bones and feathers and scribblings in black chalk on the Deanery doorstep.

'I've already been on to Double Felix at Berebury today on behalf of Canon Willoughby,' explained Barry Wright, trying not to sound too defensive, 'to arrange for some more security lighting, but I'm afraid they aren't able to deal with the matter immediately.'

'Ah,' said Malby Coton.

'I'm sorry, Mr Dean, but they said that something important has come up this morning and they're all tied up for the time being.' Wright made an effort not to sound too placatory either when he added, 'They'll come round as soon as they can, I'm sure.'

The Dean treated this remark, as he did all other communications of whatever nature, with impeccable courtesy. 'Thank you, Mr Wright.' He turned and indicated Bertram Wallingford, who was standing at his side. 'The Bishop tells me that there has been a similar – er – intrusion in the Palace garden.'

Technically and traditionally, the Bishop's house lay outside the Close, but its garden abutted the perimeter wall, a gate in the wall giving easy access to the Close and the Minster. It hadn't always been so. In fact, the gateway between the two properties had been walled up more than once over the ages, but not since 1485. It was during the Wars of the Roses when the

Dean and the Bishop had last had a major row, one having been unfortunately a Yorkist and the other a Lancastrian.

'There was the body of a garrotted rabbit on my doorstep,' said Bertie Wallingford accurately, 'amongst other things. I don't know how it got there.'

The Clerk of Works took the reference to this intrusion to be a reflection on the Minster's security system, which was also one of his manifold responsibilities, and hastened into speech. 'I've already had a word with the nightwatchmen, Mr Dean, and they were not aware of there having been any intruders in the Close last night.'

'Ah,' said Malby Coton gravely.

'But there must have been,' said the Bishop, more given to saying what he thought than the Dean.

Barry Wright said, 'The men assure me, your Grace, that they did their rounds as usual, but naturally they are unlikely to have noticed anything of – er – this particular nature, especially in the dark.' The Clerk of Works stared down uneasily at the odd collection at his feet. He was no theologian, but even he was aware that these items betokened something that was not Christian. 'One of the men did say he'd heard an odd sound very early this morning, but he didn't find anything to account for it. He thought it might have been a cat—'

'But it wasn't,' Malby Coton prompted him gently.

'No, Mr Dean?'

'No, Mr Wright. It was the bleat of a young goat in Canon Shorthouse's garden.'

'A tethered goat,' put in the Bishop. His wife had hastened back home in search of something for the goat to eat and drink.

'A goat in the garden? But', protested Wright, 'the Canon's away on a sabbatical.'

'That's right,' said the Bishop. 'He's giving the Lanenden Lectures in Paris . . .'

'To be called "The Albigensian Crusade Reconsidered",' said the Dean.

'Should be very interesting,' said the Bishop, momentarily diverted.

'The Minster,' said the Dean suddenly. 'There isn't—'

'No, Mr Dean,' Barry Wright was reassuring. 'I had that checked out first. No one's been in there that shouldn't have.' He thought again and added clumsily, 'Nor done anything in there that they shouldn't have done either.'

'That's a relief,' said Malby Coton, relaxing visibly. 'We wouldn't want to have to close the Minster and be arranging for a reconsecration at short notice.'

'Or an exorcism,' said the Bishop.

'Just as well,' said the Dean. 'Isn't Canon Shorthouse our diocesan "Deliverance from Evil" specialist these days?'

'So he is,' admitted the Bishop. 'I'd forgotten that for a moment. Don't get a lot of call for exorcism in the ordinary way. That's for the best, too, since he's abroad.'

'What we should be arranging', said the Dean in a

businesslike way, 'is a briefing for our public relations people.'

'Hush it up, you mean, Mr Dean?' said Barry Wright.

'No, no,' said Malby Coton. 'That wouldn't do at all. Get our oar in first is what I mean. Whoever's done this will soon spread it about anyway. We'll give our version to the local paper straight away and before anyone else.'

'With photographs,' added the Bishop, who had once gone to a talk on the Church and the media.

Photographs or, rather, the summoning of the police photographers, Dyson and Williams, was one of the things on the mind of Detective Inspector Sloan, too: one of the many things.

The figure on the ground was lying face down in front of the statue of the bull and it was by no means photogenic. Moreover, it was lying in a position which suggested that it had been carefully placed at the feet of the bull, rather than simply cast down in front of it.

'She's dead,' repeated Pete Carter unnecessarily. 'I keep telling everyone that she's dead.'

'Do you know who she is?' asked Sloan. There was no doubt about the woman being dead. What she had died from wasn't so immediately obvious. He noted automatically that as Captain Prosser had seemed to recognize her, then it must have been from what she was wearing, since her face was still hidden from view.

Pete Carter shook his head. 'Never set eyes on her until I turned that corner there and came into this bit of the maze.'

'Miss Pedlinge,' asked Sloan through his radio, something stirring deep down in the vestigial memories of his schooldays, 'isn't there an old legend about tributes to a bull somewhere?'

'Sacrifices, you mean,' she said promptly, her voice coming clearly over the air. 'Oh, yes indeed. The Cretan Minotaur demanded a tribute of seven youths and seven virgins . . .'

'She's not a virgin,' said Crosby, pointing at the body of the woman, 'at least, sir,' his face producing a ruddy blush, 'not if that wedding ring is anything to go by.'

'Miss Pedlinge,' said Detective Inspector Sloan into his radio telephone, 'will you please switch off now? I am going to have to ring Berebury for further assistance.'

'Over and out,' said the old lady unexpectedly before the line went dead.

Chapter Seven

'We've found the body of a woman, sir,' reported Detective Inspector Sloan over the air to Superintendent Leeyes. 'It was just where Miss Pedlinge said we would find her. Name unknown to us.'

'We've got a woman just reported missing,' barked back his superior officer. 'Name of Margaret Collins.'

'It's quite difficult to estimate her age, sir, as we can't see her face . . . not without turning her over, that is, and we can't do that until Dyson and Williams get here.' The two police photographers were on their way. 'And Dr Dabbe.' Dr Hector Smithson Dabbe was the forensic pathologist for East Calleshire and he was on his way, too. But he would beat the photographers to it. He drove more quickly than was good for him or anyone else.

'She was twenty-five last birthday,' said Leeyes. 'If she's the missing woman, that is.'

'And dead, I would say at a guess, sir, under twenty-four hours,' plodded on Sloan. 'Dr Dabbe'll tell us, of course, when he's got here.'

'And missing', came back the Superintendent

cogently, 'since yesterday afternoon . . . we've got the husband here at the station now telling us all about her not having been with their little son at the hospital overnight like he thought.'

'I see, sir,' said Detective Inspector Sloan. 'In that case a formal identification would be a great help. If,' he added as an afterthought, 'visual identification is possible. From what can be seen without touching the body, it might be that the face is damaged. There's some blood about. Not a lot.' There was something curious about the blood around the face that he had automatically registered but not yet explored in his mind.

'And the cause of death?' asked Leeyes, never one to prevaricate.

'Not immediately apparent, sir,' said Sloan cautiously.

'And what,' Leeyes asked irritably, 'in the name of all that's holy, is this woman who may or may not be Margaret Collins doing lying dead in a maze at Aumerle Court at Staple St James instead of being a good mother in the children's ward at the hospital?'

Detective Inspector Sloan turned and regarded the Minotaur and the figure lying prone in front of it. 'I couldn't say, but I understand, sir, that a load of ancient symbolism is attached to reaching the very centre of a maze and thus getting to the statue of the Minotaur . . .' He hesitated. The extent of the Superintendent's knowledge and of his ignorance were both equally unknown, and it was very dangerous to presume either. The man was an aficionado of adult education classes and he could as easily have attended one on Greek myth and legend as the one called 'French without Tears' which had kept him – and the lecturer – busy the last winter. Sloan took a deep breath and resumed his narrative. 'The Minotaur, as you know, sir, is half bull and half man.'

Something resembling a strangled snort came over the ether.

'. . . and,' hastened on Sloan, 'he – it – was said to have been the object of human sacrifice in ancient times.'

'If you ask me, Sloan,' grunted Leeyes, 'it's a load of whole bull, not half and half.'

'Yes, sir,' said Sloan. So the Superintendent hadn't done a course on Greek mythology, then. Perhaps it was just as well.

'And we are, may I remind you, Sloan, now in the early twenty-first century.'

'Yes, sir.' He looked back at the Minotaur. 'Would it be possible, sir, to have a description of the woman who has been reported missing?'

'The husband says his wife's about five foot three inches tall and slightly built.'

Sloan made a note of the height of the missing wife given by the husband.

Leeyes grunted. 'Actually this David Collins said everything in metric, but five foot three is how tall she really is.'

'Yes, sir.' So much for 'French without Tears' and the twenty-first century.

'Husbands don't always know, of course, Sloan. Can't be absolutely sure and all that. In my experience,' he said largely, 'the longer they've been married, the less well men can describe what their wives look like.'

'And what was she wearing?' asked Sloan, ignoring this tempting marital bypath. The woman in front of him fitted the physical description, all right, and that was enough for him to be going on with.

'When this fellow left his wife at the hospital yesterday afternoon,' carried on the Superintendent, 'she had on a blue cotton blouse, deeper blue jeans and summer sandals. She was carrying a white cardigan and a largish white handbag.'

The dead woman in the maze was dressed in a blue outfit and wearing a white cardigan. Perhaps, Sloan thought, she had put the cardigan on when it had turned cool. She still had one sandal on. The other was lying on the ground as if it had been kicked off by its owner. He looked around about him, turning his mouth away from the telephone connection with the Superintendent. 'Crosby, see if there's a white handbag lying about anywhere—'

'It's over there,' interrupted Pete Carter, jerking a finger. 'Saw it as soon as I got here. I haven't touched it. Mind you,' he added virtuously, 'in the ordinary way, I'd have picked it up and handed it in, like always. You'd be surprised what people leave behind in the maze . . .', he averted his eyes from the deceased, 'by accident, I mean.'

'Sloan, are you still there?' The radio started to make spluttering noises. 'Sloan, can you hear me?'

'Yes, sir.'

'And this woman had shoulder-length brown hair. Does that confirm anything?'

'In a way, sir. This woman has shoulder-length brown hair, which is why we can't see her face very well.'

'The husband,' said Superintendent Leeyes, 'seemed to think his wife'd been under rather a lot of strain lately.'

'We'll be looking into that, sir, naturally—'

'And while you're about it, Sloan, and out there in Staple St James, you can send Crosby over to Pear Tree Farm at Almstone. It'll save another journey out into the country and get him out from under your feet.'

'Sir?'

'They've had a young kid taken from the farm yesterday—'

'A child?' Sloan stiffened. An abduction was the very last thing he needed now or at any other time.

'A young goat – and they're very upset about it. Right up Crosby's street, I should have thought.' He gave the seal-like bark which did duty for his laugh. 'Getting their goat, instead of mine . . .'

* * * * *

Captain Prosser was waiting with Kenny Prickett where Sloan had left him. He was standing strained-faced but silent as the Detective Inspector and a very subdued Pete Carter emerged from the maze. Prosser tightened up his stance, bringing his heels together immediately he saw the policeman emerge.

'I shall want to interview everyone living at Aumerle Court and on the staff here,' announced Sloan baldly.

'Certainly, Inspector,' said Prosser, his eyes on Sloan's face.

'Especially anyone with access to the maze yesterday,' said Sloan.

'Found something, have you?' said Kenny Prickett informally. 'There now, I didn't think Pete here would holler for nothing. Not Pete.'

Pete was silent.

'He hasn't,' said Sloan, noticing Prosser run a tongue over dry lips. 'And I'll need that bin of yours kept untouched from now on, as well as his. The forensic scientists are going to want to examine that.'

Kenny backed away from his refuse bin as if it had been alive. 'You've found someone then—'

'And I'll have to have a proper chat with you and your mate,' said Sloan, one eye still on Jeremy Prosser. He turned and said to the estate manager, 'And with you, too, Captain Prosser, if I may . . .'

The man stiffened. 'Of course, Inspector.'

'One of the things I would like to know', said Sloan, 'is why there isn't a map of the maze available.'

'You might well ask,' said Prosser.

'Dr Dabbe,' said Sloan, 'who's our forensic pathologist, will be here any minute now and he's going
to want to get in there quickly.'

'I quite understand,' Captain Prosser said thickly,
'but it's not quite as simple as that—'

'And I would have thought', pressed on Sloan, 'that
there would have been a plan of the maze in your
files.'

'So there should have been,' replied Prosser
smartly, 'but Miss Pedlinge won't hear of it.'

'Likes to keep in charge, does Miss Daphne,'
observed Kenny Prickett.

'Miss Pedlinge', said the Captain stiffly, 'has given
me to understand that she regards the maze as her own
province.'

'Keeps all the estate papers in the Long Gallery,'
Prickett informed them, 'so that Mr Bevis can't get his
hands on them when he comes over.'

'Mr Bevis?' asked Sloan.

'Her great-nephew,' said Kenny. 'He can have
everything when she's gone, Miss Daphne says, and
not a minute before.'

'Ah,' said Sloan, tucking the name away in his
mind.

'I have also been given to understand that Mr Bevis
is Miss Pedlinge's heir,' put in Captain Prosser.

'I see,' said Sloan.

'He's a bit of a lad,' said Kenny Prickett. 'Always
was.'

'I see,' said Detective Inspector Sloan again, adding Bevis Pedlinge to his mental list of those to be interviewed.

'Always liked being in charge has Miss Daphne,' repeated Kenny conversationally. 'Ever since I was a boy, anyway. Knows her own mind, does Miss Daphne.' He turned to Pete Carter. 'Doesn't she, mate?'

'Yes.' Carter nodded. He seemed stunned by what he had found and unwilling to speak further.

'I have to say that Miss Pedlinge does know the maze like the back of her hand,' admitted the Captain, 'and although I have several times expressed a willingness to draw up proper working plans of it she has always indicated—'

Kenny Prickett chortled. 'Indicated! Miss Daphne! That's good, that is. Miss Daphne's not one to indicate. She always calls a spade a bloomin' shovel.'

'. . . made clear, then,' Prosser swiftly rephrased this, 'that she would prefer me not to undertake the exercise.'

'Like I said,' Prickett grinned, 'Miss Daphne knows her own mind. And she doesn't like change either.'

'And I shall also need to know', swept on Sloan, 'about how access is ordinarily obtained to the grounds and Aumerle Court.'

'The house closes to visitors at five o'clock in the summer,'said the agent, 'but members of the public are allowed to walk in the grounds until dusk.'

'I meant how are people let in and kept out?' In

what passed for his spare time Detective Inspector Sloan was a gardener, specializing in growing roses. It was a hobby that went with shift work. And there was a horticultural expression lurking at the back of Sloan's mind that covered enclosed gardens – it would come back to him in a moment – *hortus inclusus*, that was what it was. With a bit of luck, the grounds of Aumerle Court might constitute a *hortus inclusus* and thus make life easier for a pair of busy policemen. For one busy policeman, anyway. He didn't suppose for one moment that Detective Constable Crosby was doing anything except stand guard over the body of a woman.

'They have to come in by the main gate, where they pay—' began Prosser.

'Although there's a tradesman's entrance round the back,' Kenny Prickett added, 'where you don't.'

'That's the postern gate,' explained Prosser. 'It leads to the back of the Court and the old stables and so forth.'

'And to the tea garden and the shop, as well,' said Kenny Prickett, continuing gratuitously, 'where most of the money is made.' He nudged Pete Carter. 'That's right, mate, isn't it?'

'Yes,' said Carter, still monosyllabic.

'And the men's bothy is there,' added Captain Prosser. 'That's where they keep all their tools. That's behind the stable yard.'

'Where it doesn't lower the tone of the place,' said Kenny Prickett, straight-faced. 'Not that we're around

much any longer on Sundays, Pete and me. No overtime, these days, you see.'

Captain Prosser's face turned a ripe shade of red,
but he kept silent. Pete Carter stood unresponsive at
his mate's side.

'And when do the staff come off the gate and the
maze?' asked Sloan.

'Five o'clock,' said Prosser.

'Sharp,' added Prickett.

The other men looked at him.

'Everything's sharp here,' said Prickett pointedly.
'Isn't it, Mr Prosser?'

'Punctuality helps oil the world's wheels,' said the
soldier.

'And how, may I ask,' enquired Sloan, 'can you be
sure that there's no one left in the maze when you all
go home?'

'We count them in,' began Prosser.

'And we count them out,' chanted Kenny Prickett.

'And?' said Sloan.

'And if the numbers don't tally,' said Prosser, 'we
ask Miss Pedlinge to check.' He gave a thin smile. 'She
likes that.'

'One evening she caught a couple in her binoculars
canoodling under the statue of that fancy lad in there,'
chortled Kenny Prickett.

'Androgeos,' said Captain Prosser.

'They wanted to stay there all night,' said Kenny,
giving a loud cackle. 'Found that Androgeos an
inspiration, I daresay.' He grinned. 'Reckoned without

Miss Daphne and her long-look glasses, didn't they? Soon winkled them out.'

'The postern gate,' said Detective Inspector Sloan, rising above this and unerringly putting his finger on the weakest security spot, 'when is that locked?'

'That's locked to vehicles at five o'clock, too,' said Captain Prosser. 'The pedestrian access gets locked last thing at night by Milly Smithers when she goes home.'

'She puts Miss Daphne to bed,' volunteered Kenny, 'and opens up first thing in the morning when she comes in to get her up.'

Detective Inspector Sloan noted the information with relief. Fixed points of reference were always a help in a police investigation.

There was another fixed point of reference worth exploring, too.

'Perhaps you'd take me over to see Miss Pedlinge again,' he said to Jeremy Prosser.

A woman with nothing to do but look out of a window could be a great help in any investigation, but her probity as a witness would have to be established, too. With her history she might well have been trained in misinformation, let alone disinformation.

Besides, an old lady at odds with an heir was someone to be watched in her own right. But there was something else about the elderly that Sloan had been trained to keep in mind; their increasing indifference to matters of supreme importance to the young and the middle-aged. As his old station Sergeant had been fond of reminding him, 'Age and treachery will always overcome youth and skill.'

Chapter Eight

Sharon Gibbons took one look at David Collins's expression as he came through the door of Double Felix and disappeared back into her own office, murmuring, 'Coffee coming up, pronto.'

'I must say I could use it,' admitted Collins, slumping down at his desk and running his hands through his hair. 'It's been one hell of a morning, Eric.'

'What news?' asked his partner, never a man to waffle.

'Margaret wasn't at the hospital,' said Collins, pushing a pile of notebooks to one side with a hand that was not entirely steady.

'Wasn't she?' Paterson said absent-mindedly.

Collins shook his head. 'She hasn't been there since yesterday afternoon.'

'That's bad.'

'I did wonder to begin with if she'd gone over to her mother's—'

'But she hadn't?' Eric finished for him.

'No.' He took a deep breath and said thickly, 'The

good news is that Mr Beaumont, the consultant at the hospital, seems happy enough with James for the time being, but there's no sign of Margaret.'

'None?'

'None anywhere, Eric.'

'And no word?'

Collins shook his head. 'Not a dicky bird. The hospital think she slipped away from the ward sometime yesterday afternoon, but they're not exactly sure when. Not that they're likely to have noticed especially, anyway, they're so pressed on the children's ward – particularly at the weekend.'

'No letter?' asked Eric Paterson swiftly.

'That's the first thing the police asked, too,' said David Collins wearily. 'And the answer is not that I could see. I don't suppose I'd have noticed anything when I got back from the Minster last night, but I had a damned good look when I went home from the hospital this morning after I found out that she hadn't been there all night and before I went to the police.'

'Nothing?'

'Not a thing.' He opened his hands in a gesture of despair. 'No note, nothing missing from the house, no message on the answerphone—'

'People don't just disappear into thin air,' frowned Paterson.

'Coffee,' announced Sharon Gibbons.

'What? Oh, thanks.' He turned and absently picked up the mug.

Usually the secretary hung about in the partners'

room as long as she could to catch whatever gossip was going, but there was something in the atmosphere today that made her retreat to her own office as soon as she could.

'What about James?' asked Eric, exercising as usual his unerring eye for essentials.

'The hospital is keeping him, thank goodness, until Margaret's mother gets here,' said David. 'She's on her way over now.'

'That'll help,' said Eric Paterson.

'The going was tough enough as it was without Margaret taking off, I can tell you.' Collins sank his face towards the mug of coffee. 'God, I needed that. Thirsty work, talking to the police.'

'What did they say?'

David Collins essayed a tired smile. 'They asked all the questions you just have, Eric, but in a different order. They wanted to know how Margaret had been lately, too.'

'Naturally.' Eric Paterson did not add that he could see how the police mind was working.

'Well, how would you be if your only child was suffering in the way our little James has been?'

'In a very poor way,' said Eric Paterson immediately. It had always been hard work to get him near even a doctor, let alone a hospital.

'They wanted to know if she'd been showing any signs of stress.' He snorted. 'Stress! I ask you, Eric! Of course, she was stressed out. We both are.'

'Sleepless?'

'I don't suppose we've had a good night since James was first diagnosed. Either of us.' He paused and said awkwardly, 'It wasn't only James we had to worry about either.' He went on obliquely 'It's all very well for the doctors to talk in percentages but statistics aren't everything—'

'As the chap said who was drowned in a river whose average depth was six inches,' said Eric with an attempt at lightness. 'Sorry, David, go on.'

'Hereditary diseases don't only affect the next generation, you know.' He plunged his face into the coffee mug. 'We had a lot to think about, both of us.'

Eric Paterson looked distinctly uncomfortable. 'Did you tell the police that you'd been snipped?'

'I didn't think my vasectomy was anything to do with them,' David Collins said with dignity. 'Besides, Margaret was all in favour of my having it done. She said she couldn't go through all this again with another child, and I know I couldn't.'

'No, no,' Eric agreed hastily, changing the subject. 'So what are you going to do now?'

For the first time a quiver crept into the other man's voice. 'I couldn't bear to go home and just sit and wait for news, Eric. I said to the police that I'd come back here and get on with some work.'

'Only if you really want to,' said his partner. 'We can manage, you know.'

'But I shan't be able to manage if I haven't anything to do,' said Collins, strain showing in every line of his face.

'Well, they'll know where to find you,' agreed Paterson gruffly.

'In fact, I might just nip over to the Minster and finish off last night's job. That'll give me something to do.'

'Good idea. They want you back over there anyway.' Eric Paterson pawed through the pile of files on his desk. 'There's a message here from them somewhere. They've got more trouble there this morning.'

His partner didn't respond directly. Instead he said, 'You know, Eric, I could have sworn I heard a goat bleating while I was working in the slype yesterday evening.'

'I expect the Dean had separated it from the sheep,' Eric said solemnly. 'Isn't that what the clergy are for?'

'Thought you'd be back, Inspector,' observed Miss Daphne Pedlinge with patent satisfaction. She lowered her binoculars and gave her wheelchair a quarter-turn in Sloan's direction. 'Well?'

He had his notebook open in an instant. 'I need some timings from you.'

'Nothing like having good anchor bearings, is there?' she said.

'Or a reliable witness,' said Sloan, not at all sure what anchor bearings were.

That pleased the old lady. 'The gates close to those visitors coming in at five pip emma,' she responded without prompting. 'And I hoist the all-clear signal for the maze as soon as possible after that.'

'How exactly?' He wouldn't have been overwhelmingly surprised to find a flagpole protruding from her window.

Miss Pedlinge pointed to a long cord hanging down from a window blind. 'I lower that curtain – they can see that from the gate. They know then that everyone's out of the grounds as well as the maze and that they can shut up shop for the day.'

'Therefore you yourself can't see anything from here afterwards unless you pull the window blind up again,' he concluded aloud, indicating the broad sweep of the grounds visible from her eyrie.

'True.' She gave a little shrug. 'But then, Inspector, in the ordinary way there's usually nothing to see and so I stand down.' She gave him a shrewd look. 'But we aren't in the ordinary way today, are we?'

He shook his head.

'Thought not,' she said. 'I still know a dead body when I see one. That war poet was wrong, you know, when he shook a soldier friend awake in his dugout because when he slept he reminded him of the dead.'

'Poetic licence,' said Sloan.

'Siegfried Sassoon, that was,' she said reminiscently. 'Mind you, he must have known really.'

'Like you did,' Sloan reminded her.

'You can usually tell—'

'With practice,' said the policeman.

'Yes, indeed.' She sighed.

'But that also means,' he got back to the point,

leaving her concurrence in the matter of the easy recognition of death unexplored for the time being, 'that until you lower the window blind you yourself can always tell if there is anyone still in there – after closing time or not.'

'Oh, yes, Inspector, you can be sure of that.' She gave a sardonic chuckle. 'And quite often there is. You'd be quite surprised at what the young think they can get away with these days.'

Detective Inspector Sloan, working policeman, didn't think he would – or could – any longer be surprised by anything that today's young got up to, but he didn't say so. Instead he said, 'And you didn't see anyone – or anything – out of the ordinary at all over there yesterday evening?'

'Not after closing time,' she said without hesitation.

'Even though it wasn't dark until much later?'

'Not a thing after five pip emma,' she repeated, adding with the altered values of the old, 'Besides, it was my teatime.'

'Does anyone – Captain Prosser, for instance – report to you at the end of the day?'

She gave a grim chuckle. 'Inspector, the only person who reports to me after that is Milly Smithers and she only comes in to give me my supper and put me to bed.'

Sloan made a note.

She patted the arms of her wheelchair. 'Don't grow old, Inspector. It's not worth it.'

'There are those, miss, who think that the alternative is worse.' Some there were who didn't, of course. Unfortunately some of those who thought death preferable to an impaired life were working in the caring professions. From time to time this became a worry to Sloan and his Criminal Investigation Department, not to say to some relatives of those whose quality of life was debatable.

But not all relatives, which was a worry of another sort altogether.

'At least,' offered Daphne Pedlinge philosophically, 'that young woman lying out there dead now knows for certain which is better, even if we don't.'

'Perhaps,' he said. 'Or perhaps not.' Either way, there was a certain nursing home in one of the villages in which he wouldn't like his own mother ever to be a patient. 'Tell me, how long has the Captain worked here?'

'A year, perhaps. Almost, anyway.'

'And before that?'

She waved a hand. 'He was with the Ornums over at Almstone, but they had to retrench and we needed someone here at the time.'

'We?'

'My great-nephew and I. For better or worse Bevis appointed him.' She pursed her lips. 'I agreed on the old principle of better the devil you know—'

'So you knew him anyway?'

'I didn't. Bevis did – he's a neighbour of his at Nether Hoystings.'

'Near Calleford,' said Sloan.

'Near the main railway line,' said Miss Pedlinge. 'Bevis has to go up to town every day to earn his crust. Until I die, that is. In the meantime—'

'Yes?' Detective Inspector Sloan's Criminal Investigation Department had a vested interest in all situations that were changed by death.

'Bevis has to help keep this place going – and his wife and children,' she added by way of an afterthought. 'They cost too, of course, and perhaps in the end more than they should.'

'I see.' He would cause enquiries to be made later at Almstone and Nether Hoystings about Captain Prosser, who had not only recognized the deceased but had seen fit not to tell the police that he had. And find out whether a wife and children costing more than they should was the natural reaction to domesticity of an elderly spinster with a small stately home to keep going.

'Of course, he'll live here when I'm dead,' said Miss Pedlinge with equanimity, 'and, God and government willing, his sons and grandsons, too.'

'And does – Bevis, did you say? – come over here at weekends?' Sloan had no idea how wide a net he would have to cast to embrace all who knew their way into the centre of the maze at Aumerle Court, but presumably a younger Bevis Pedlinge would have worked his way round it as a boy. And, once mastered, could have remembered the layout.

'Often enough,' she said ambiguously. She gave her

wheelchair a sudden turn away from him and looked out of the window. 'Sundays, usually.'

'Like yesterday?'

'He was here in the afternoon,' she said, turning her head. 'Did you know, Inspector, that there's someone else trying to get into the maze? Tall, grey-haired, proper suit, with a man carrying a big black bag following him.' She grinned. 'And Kenny Prickett isn't letting him in—'

'The pathologist!' exclaimed Sloan.

'That was quick.'

'Fastest driver in Calleshire, bar none,' said Sloan. 'I must go.'

'But you *did* hear a goat, Mr Collins,' said the Bishop, as David Collins began to load some of his electrical equipment on to his van in the Close. 'It's still in Canon Shorthouse's garden. And still bleating, too.'

The lighting expert gave an uneasy laugh 'It was quite creepy enough, anyway, I can tell you, sir, in the slype in the half dark, without odd noises in the middle distance.'

Bertram Wallingford nodded. 'You know, sometimes when I'm sitting in my own garden and looking across at the Minster I can get quite overcome by the weight of the past myself.'

'The Dean thought it was high time the slype was lit properly,' put in Barry Wright, the Clerk of Works carefully. Strictly speaking, the Minster building was no concern of the Bishop of Calleford, even though it was the focal point of his diocese. A practical man himself, Barry Wright had no time for fanciful ideas about the past either. What mattered to him about days gone by was whether the medieval craftsmen had done their work in the Minster and the Close well or not. If they hadn't – or if it was time-expired – then that just meant more work for him now: historical romance didn't come into it.

'It was quite a relief to see you, sir, and the Dean go by after the service yesterday evening,' admitted Collins to the Bishop, oblivious to the finer points of ecclesiastical law.

'I must say I didn't hear a goat or anything else myself as we went past,' said Wallingford, 'but then my wife is always telling me that I'm getting deaf.'

'And you were both talking, sir,' ventured Collins lightly.

'I dare say we were.' The Bishop waved a hand to encompass the whole Minster Close. 'There's always something going on in a place like this that seems important at the time, if not in the judgement of history.'

Barry Wright, who considered the Close nothing but a hothouse of gossip and intrigue, put his oar in again. He had, after all, his own corner to mind. 'The Bishop', he explained to David Collins, 'also wants some security lighting in his garden and over his porch but, you understand, this will be a matter for the diocese rather than the Minster authorities.'

'Received and understood,' David Collins acknowledged the message with a quick jerk of his head. Customers with turf wars were something that the firm of Double Felix Ltd understood only too well. More important than turf wars, though, was new business, so he pointed to Canon Shorthouse's house. 'Will there be anything needed there, too, in the nature of special security lighting, since there seems to have been some trouble over at the Canonry as well?'

'I suppose you'd better give me an estimate while you're here,' allowed Wright grudgingly. 'The Canon will want to know all about the goat and what we've done about it when he gets back.'

'I'll take a look-see when I've tied up a few loose ends in the slype,' said Collins. 'There's still a little to be done there. I didn't quite finish yesterday.'

'Don't forget us, though, will you?' said the Bishop. 'My wife is most anxious that there shouldn't be a repetition of last night's – er – highly undesirable activities.'

Barry Wright, who preferred plain speaking to euphemism, merely said that someone from the Calleshire Animal Sanctuary over at Edsway would be along very soon to take care of the goat. 'A Miss Alison Kirk', he said, consulting a file, 'has been asked by the police to take it into protective custody for the time being.'

'Right then,' said David Collins, squaring his shoulders, 'I'd better be getting on now—'

Barry Wright walked part of the way over to the

slype with him. 'They said at your office that you wouldn't be back this morning because of a problem—' he began curiously.

The other man looked at him with a certain distaste. 'Nothing that can't be handled, thank you.'

David Collins's stiff upper lip though lasted only until he bumped into the Bishop's wife. When Mrs Wallingford asked kindly after both his wife Margaret and little James, his face crumpled and he told her everything.

'All you can do now', she said simply, 'is to keep busy and pray.'

Chapter Nine

'Yes,' said David Collins dully, emitting a deep sigh and swaying a little, 'that's my wife Margaret, all right.'

The man had been collected from the Minster at Calleford by Detective Constable Crosby and brought over to the viewing room at the mortuary at Berebury. He had taken one swift look through the protective glass window at the body lying there, the bruised face now clearly visible, and then quickly turned away.

'Do you think I could possibly sit down somewhere, please?' he said to Detective Inspector Sloan, looking round for a chair. 'It's all been a bit of a shock.'

Sloan led the way back to the waiting room, where Collins sank down on a chair, his head between his hands.

'I can't say I'm surprised,' he admitted presently to Detective Inspector Sloan, lifting his head a little. 'Not after I heard she'd gone missing.'

'Really, sir?' said Sloan at his most encouraging.

Collins moistened his lips. 'I've always been a bit

afraid that she might do something like this. Since James was ill, I mean.'

'Ah,' Detective Inspector Sloan nodded sympathetically.

'You've no idea of the strain we've been under, Inspector,' he said, his face starting to crumple again. 'Nobody could possibly imagine what it's like who hasn't been through it themselves . . .'

'Quite so,' said Sloan, clearing his throat. 'Do you think you might be able to give us some help on timing? For the record,' he added sedulously.

'I can't help a lot,' David Collins managed to say. He seemed to be having some difficulty in forming his words. With a visible effort he struggled into speech. 'I left Margaret at the hospital just before half-past two yesterday afternoon – they try to get the children to sleep after lunch, although it doesn't work with all of them . . .'

'Naturally.' It always worked with Superintendent Leeyes, although nobody at the police station ever acknowledged the fact. Any member of the Force below the rank of Commander who disturbed him after lunch did so at their peril.

'And that was the last time I saw her,' finished Collins uncertainly, lowering his head again. 'Poor Margaret.'

'I see, sir,' said Sloan. 'And after that?'

'I don't know what she did after that, Inspector. The hospital couldn't tell me.'

'And what did you do?' asked Sloan in a tone

completely devoid of emphasis. Sporting rules about not hitting a man when he was down didn't apply to police questioning. You caught your subject when he – or she – was at his most vulnerable. Sitting targets might be too easy for sportsmen, but they were easier for detectives to hit than moving ones. Only he didn't know whether David Collins was quarry or not.

Yet.

'Me?' the man answered indifferently, 'Oh, I went over to Aumerle Court first to check out the maze there. They're planning to have a sound and light exhibition in the grounds as soon as it's dark enough in the early evening and I was taking some measurements in there for the wiring circuits and so forth.'

'On a Sunday?'

'The owner's great-nephew only comes down at weekends,' he said. 'We needed to talk about the lighting arrangements for the performance.'

'No peace for the wicked,' said Detective Constable Crosby from the sidelines.

Sloan, who had been judging to a nicety the point at which he could go into the question of David Collins's other movements decided against saying anything more. Crosby he would deal with later.

Collins, though, seemed not to have heard the Constable. 'The old lady over there seems to be some sort of control freak—'

'You can say that again,' muttered Crosby under his breath.

'So Jeremy Prosser advised me just to slip in there

with the paying customers while I sussed the place out. So I did.'

'And then?'

'Then I met up with Jeremy – Captain Prosser, that is – and Mr Bevis.' His head suddenly went down between his hands again. 'How am I going to tell Margaret's mother?'

'Difficult,' agreed Sloan. 'It's always very difficult, that. And then?'

'What? Oh, then we talked about what would need to be done before they could start rehearsals – that sort of thing. After we'd all finished Jeremy offered me some tea, but I wanted to get over to Calleford Minster – besides, I had a Thermos in the van. And Mr Bevis had to report back to his aunt.'

'That figures,' said Crosby.

But Margaret Collins's husband had lost interest in his own narrative. 'What happens next?' he asked bleakly.

'An examination to establish the cause of death by the pathologist,' said Sloan, avoiding the word autopsy. 'The Coroner's officer will be in touch. By the way,' he added casually, 'you spoke as if you knew Captain Prosser—'

'But I do,' said Collins readily. 'That's how Double Felix comes to be doing the work at Aumerle Court. Jeremy's a neighbour of ours over at Nether Hoy-stings.' A stricken look suddenly came over his face as a new thought struck him. 'Oh, God! The neighbours—'

'Don't worry,' said Detective Inspector Sloan out of a lifetime of working in the police force. 'This sort of news travels very fast.'

Milly Smithers stood poised in the doorway of the Long Gallery of Aumerle Court. 'Would you be wanting anything else, Miss Daphne, before I go downstairs and start to get dinner?'

'Just my telephone book, Milly, thank you.' Daphne Pedlinge laid her binoculars down on her knee rug. 'I don't think there'll be anything to watch outside for a bit.'

'I'm sure I hope not, indeed.' Milly sounded quite indignant. 'There's been quite enough excitement out there to be going on with.'

'Yes, Milly,' said the old lady with uncharacteristic meekness. She waited until the carer had gone before she picked up her cordless telephone and flipped through a list. She tapped out a London number.

'United Mellemetics,' said a voice at the other end. 'Can I help you?'

'I wish to speak to the Assistant Head of Corporate Affairs,' said Daphne Pedlinge, 'Human Resources Division.'

'Just one moment, please.' Then, 'I'm putting you through now.'

'Mr Bevis Pedlinge's' office,' said a young female voice.

'I want to speak to him, please.'

'I'm sorry, but he's in a meeting.'

'Then get him out of it,' said Miss Pedlinge in a tone that long ago had commanded instant attention closely followed by absolute obedience.

'May I ask who's calling?' countered the young female voice.

'Tell him', she ordered, 'that his great-aunt wishes to speak to him.'

The voice faltered. 'His great-aunt, did you say?'

'Daphne Pedlinge.'

The voice capitulated. 'Hold on and I'll get him for you.'

She didn't have to wait long.

'Aunt Daphne? Is that you?' asked a breathless Bevis Pedlinge.

'Well, it's hardly likely to be someone else impersonating me, is it?'

'It could have been Milly ringing on your behalf.' Bevis always resolved not to be steam-rollered by his great-aunt and always was.

'Ha!' she pounced. 'What you hoped was that it was Milly ringing to tell you that I'd croaked it at last.'

'No, I wasn't,' he protested.

'You surprise me,' she said acidly. 'Well, I've got another sort of surprise for you.'

'Tell me—'

'We've got a body in the maze.'

'What? A dead body, you mean?'

'Of course I mean a dead body, Bevis. I wouldn't

have rung you otherwise. You aren't out to lunch already, are you?'

'Of course not.'

'I was speaking figuratively,' she said. 'And what's the meaning of your job title? In my day,' she grumbled, 'we had men and materials, not human resources. I don't know what the world is coming to.'

'Aunt Daphne,' he interrupted her, 'what sort of a dead body?'

'Female,' she said.

'But who?'

'Ah, that's what nobody knows yet.'

'But I was in the maze myself yesterday afternoon.'

'Nobody knows that either, Bevis. Yet. But they will. And pretty soon, too. You can be sure of that. So . . .' Daphne Pedlinge carefully put the telephone down while she was in the middle of speaking herself.

That, she had found over the years, always confused everybody nicely.

'Yes, I'm Dr Dilys Chomel,' agreed the young House Surgeon when the two policemen had finally tracked her down to the children's ward at the Berebury and District General Hospital. 'When did I last see Mrs Margaret Collins? It would have been sometime yesterday afternoon – today's Monday isn't it?'

Detective Inspector Sloan nodded. He'd often found that people who worked weekends or nights didn't always know which day of the week it was, and this girl looked tired enough to have forgotten more than that.

'We get a lot of visitors on this ward on Sunday afternoons,' she said, adding unenthusiastically, 'especially fathers, which doesn't help.'

Sloan raised an enquiring eyebrow.

'Fathers always want things spelling out more,' she said wearily. 'Somehow mothers seem to know the answers without asking.'

'And the children?' asked Crosby, staring uneasily at a preternaturally bald child playing with a giant teddy bear. He'd been planning that sort of haircut himself, but he decided against it rather quickly now.

'Oh, the children don't worry half so much as you'd think because, of course,' she carried on with painful honesty, 'they're still young enough to think that we know all the answers and that we're going to get them better soon.'

'And you don't?' suggested Detective Constable Crosby. Crosby did not like hospitals any more than he liked attending post-mortems. He liked seeing sick children, though, even less, especially very sick ones. Nor did the deceptively cheerful lemon-coloured decor and ample supply of toys on the children's ward raise his spirits one little bit.

'We don't know quite everything about James's trouble,' admitted Dr Chomel, 'although I suppose that goes for many serious conditions. And as for getting him better . . .', she shrugged her shoulders, 'it's still too early to say, though we're quite optimistic at this stage.'

'But you talked to Mrs Collins about her child yesterday all the same?' said Detective Inspector Sloan, who had not for one moment forgotten the object of their visit to the hospital.

'Of course I did,' responded the doctor. 'The poor woman was worried stiff about James and no wonder.' She pointed to the end of the ward, where a little boy with one eye bandaged was engaged in the systematic destruction of a model car, and opened her hands in a gesture of despair, 'But telling parents that their little one has had to lose an eye at this age—'

'Difficult,' agreed Detective Inspector Sloan, who in his time had had to break much less palatable news to families about their sons.

'Mind you,' she said, automatically pulling herself up and resuming her professional mantle of careful optimism and encouragement, 'most people can manage very well with monocular vision.'

'Oh,' said Crosby, light dawning, 'so that's why they call them binoculars.'

'And, after all, losing an eye isn't the end of the world,' she said, intent, like all doctors, on minimizing other people's disasters. 'We mustn't forget that.'

'Didn't do King Harold a lot of good, though, did it?' said Detective Constable Crosby.

'Really?' said the young doctor politely. Dr Chomel had been born in Africa and her interest in European history began somewhat later than William the Conqueror.

'That's when he lost the Battle of Hastings,' said Crosby.

'Ah . . .'

'He's the one that had an arrow in his eye,' Crosby informed her.

'Let us hope, Doctor,' interposed Sloan swiftly, 'that your treatment has done the trick with little James.'

'We hope so,' sighed Dr Chomel. 'The earlier that the treatment's started the better, of course, and we think this case has been caught in time.'

'And the exact nature of James's trouble is . . .?' asked Sloan. James's father, David Collins, had given his permission for the police to ask the doctors whatever they wanted to know, merely expressing the mumbled hope that they would understand the answers better than he did. James's mother was no longer alive to be asked about anything: especially whether she had found the strain of James's illness altogether too much to bear.

'Retinoblastoma,' responded Dr Chomel promptly.

'Ah,' said Sloan, looking with new respect at the young doctor. Being so fluent in English was quite something, but being as fluent in medical English as she was, was something very different. It was a new language to him, too. 'Perhaps you'd be kind enough to spell that out for me.'

'It's the commonest intraocular tumour of child-hood,' she said when he'd written it down.

Crosby winced. 'Does that mean there's a lot of it about?'

'Not really,' the doctor said. 'One baby in every twenty thousand suffers from it.' She smiled faintly 'That's what I think you could call long odds.'

'There's nothing that statistics don't make worse, said Detective Inspector Sloan briskly. 'Nothing at all. Now what causes this . . . thing?'

'James has got the inherited form,' said Dr Chomel. 'It's an autosomal dominant condition.'

'Really?' said Detective Inspector Sloan. His own introduction to inherited diseases had come from seeing Ibsen's play *Ghosts*, but he didn't think this was the same. 'And Mrs Collins knew this?' There was something his own mother had been fond of quoting from the Bible – the Old Testament, for sure – about the sins of the fathers being visited on their sons, which didn't seem quite to fit the bill here, but had fitted *Ghosts*. He would have to think about that later.

'She did afterwards,' said Dr Chomel. 'That was part of the trouble '

'Trouble?' queried Detective Inspector Sloan, his head coming up like that of a bloodhound sniffing a scent.

'There was a whole load of guilt washing about in the family,' said the young doctor moderately. 'Knowing that the child had inherited the disease from either herself or her husband. Inevitable, I suppose.' She hesitated. 'I can tell you that it worried Mrs Collins a lot – watching James suffer from something that one of them had given him.'

'Not easy,' agreed Sloan. 'Even though there was

97

obviously no intention of inflicting harm.' The 'guilty mind' was the acid test in police work. Someone who was killed by another, who had not intended to do so, had not been murdered – and that went for the victims of crimes committed by those not responsible for their actions. They were still dead, of course, but that was something different.

'It was one of the things we talked about yesterday,' she said awkwardly. 'I tried to explain that as the disease wasn't something that either of them had intended to pass on – or could even have known about – they shouldn't try to shoulder the blame for James having it, but I don't think she really listened.'

Something in this caught Detective Constable Crosby's wayward attention. He suddenly launched into Latin. 'Not a case of mens rea, then,' he said brightly.

'Mens rea?' she echoed uncertainly.

'That's what the lawyers call that, don't they?' the Constable said. 'An evil intention behind the action. They didn't have that, the parents.'

'Mens rea means having a guilty mind,' explained Sloan to the doctor, 'or a knowledge of the wrongfulness of the act. It's important in some legal cases.'

'Not breaking the speed limit,' put in Detective Constable Crosby, whose great ambition it was to be transferred to Traffic Division. 'It doesn't help that you didn't mean to do it then. If you've been speeding, it's open and shut.'

'The parents couldn't have known,' the doctor

said seriously, sticking to what she knew and understood, 'not unless it had been present in either family before.'

'I suppose, then, that it therefore follows', said Detective Inspector Sloan ineluctably, 'that in due course James could pass on those genes, too.'

'There would be a risk, of course,' she said uneasily. 'And that was another of the things which was upsetting poor Mrs Collins yesterday.'

'I should say so,' burst out Crosby.

Yesterday was what had been in Detective Inspector Sloan's mind all along, but he did not say so.

'But it would be a quantifiable risk,' insisted the doctor.

'So's the Lottery,' remarked Crosby.

'As presumably would be the chances of the Collinses having another child with the same condition,' said Sloan, anxious to get the matter clear in his own mind, at the same time as hoping that Superintendent Leeyes would not want it explained in too much detail.

'Shutting the stable door after the horse has bolted, if you ask me,' muttered Detective Crosby under his breath.

The doctor nodded. 'There is always a small risk, but as you may imagine genetic counselling is notoriously difficult in this field,' she said. 'And you need highly sophisticated DNA analysis to do it properly.'

'I'm sure,' said Sloan warmly.

99

'That may have been done, of course,' said the girl. 'I wouldn't necessarily have been informed about that. It would have been between Mr Collins and his own doctor.'

Crosby had lost interest altogether after the mention of DNA.

'Both parents were given genetic counselling as soon as James's condition was diagnosed, though it isn't easy.' She hesitated. 'I don't think I am in a position to say more than that . . .' She looked round as a banshee wail came from a small girl who had spotted the approach of a hypodermic needle. 'I'm afraid you'll have to excuse me,' she said.

'We can go too now, sir, can't we?' said Detective Constable Crosby anxiously.

'I did suggest Mrs Collins saw her own doctor,' called Dr Chomel over her shoulder as she hurried away, 'about getting some sleeping tablets.'

Chapter Ten

'We had to let the husband go earlier,' explained Superintendent Leeyes regretfully when Sloan got back to the police station in Berebury.

'He was only reporting Margaret Collins missing, sir,' said Detective Inspector Sloan fairly. 'Nothing more.'

'That's as may be,' said Leeyes.

'Quite so, sir,' said Sloan. He forbore to remind the Superintendent that merely reporting anything was not yet a chargeable offence in anyone's eyes but his. Not in England, anyway. He couldn't answer for some police states.

'You'd better take this,' said Leeyes, waving a piece of paper in front of him. 'You'll need it.'

Sloan read over the written report of what David Collins had told the police about his wife's disappearance.

Leeyes sniffed. 'The man said he was going back to work and that they'd know where to find him if we wanted him.'

'They did know,' said Sloan. 'We wanted him to take a look at the body of this woman who's been found in the maze at Aumerle Court.'

'No grounds to detain him on, of course,' carried on the Superintendent, for whom it was axiomatic that all husbands were guilty of killing their deceased wives unless it could be demonstrated otherwise. 'Not at this stage anyway.'

'We had every reason, though, to suppose that the body found in the maze is that of his wife,' said Sloan, 'in that she answers to his description of her.' He had taken a conscious decision to bide his time before he conducted an indepth interview with Captain Prosser. One military aphorism that he was sure about was that time spent in reconnaissance was seldom wasted. 'But we needed a positive identification as soon as possible, sir, and we got it from the husband. Dr Dabbe is on his way back to the hospital now to do the post-mortem.'

Leeyes grunted. 'And what does our friendly neighbourhood pathologist have to say so far?'

'Dr Dabbe isn't willing, sir, to be dogmatic about the time of death until after he's performed the post-mortem.'

Superintendent Leeyes puffed out his cheeks. 'You won't ever catch him being helpful, Sloan.' The Superintendent suspected the opinions of all specialists on principle.

'But he's prepared to narrow it down to after the victim was last seen alive.' He didn't know yet whether the woman was a victim of someone else or herself – or just of intolerable pressure.

'And to just before she was found dead, I suppose, as usual?' interrupted Leeyes sardonically.

'And to over twelve hours ago,' finished Sloan patiently. It meant that the woman had been dead before ten o'clock that night before, which it was helpful, in police terms, to know.

'That means we're talking about yesterday, Sloan.'

'Sunday,' agreed Sloan, not sure where this was leading.

'Bad day for family relationships, Sunday,' opined the Superintendent. His own Sundays were invariably spent on the golf course. 'If the woman was driven over the edge, that is.'

'We can't say about that yet, sir.'

'How did Dr Dabbe get in and out of the maze without being airborne?'

'Dyson and Williams solved that one for us, sir.' The two men were the police photographers. 'They had a tall ladder with them. Apparently they never travel without it. We could all see where we were going a treat after that.' He had already realized both that there must have been tall ladders around at Aumerle Court when the yew was cut and, more importantly, that Captain Prosser had not seen fit to mention the fact to the police.

Nor, come to that, had the two workmen, who presumably did the cutting. It was something else to think about and he made a mental note of the fact.

'By the way, Sloan,' said Leeyes, 'you can stand Crosby down. That goat that was stolen out Staple St James way,' he looked down at his desk, 'name of Aries . . . funny name for a goat—'

'Someone's pet, then,' deduced Sloan without difficulty. 'And a ram.'

'Really? I don't know how you can tell. Well, it's been found safe and sound – but a bit hungry – over at the Minster in Calleford. Tethered in the garden of one of the houses in the Close.'

'Someone's idea of a joke, I suppose,' said Detective Inspector Sloan wearily. Jokes never went down well with policemen busy on weightier matters such as death and detection.

'What we have to be grateful for, Sloan,' said Police Superintendent Leeyes with deep feeling, 'is that the animal rights' activists do not appear to have been involved.'

'Yes, indeed,' said Sloan, deciding not to mention those who took against anthropomorphology and thus the naming of animals. He had too much on his mind just now to worry about either a goat called Aries or people who thought attributing human characteristics and names to pet animals demeaned the creature. Besides, down in the cells they had some prisoners whose behaviour wouldn't have been countenanced by any right-thinking goat. 'I'll tell Crosby that, sir. We're going over to the post-mortem now.'

'Do come along in, gentlemen,' said Dr Dabbe, the consultant pathologist to the Berebury and District General Hospital, welcoming Sloan and Crosby to the mortuary there, 'and we'll see what we can tell you about the deceased, won't we, Burns?'

Burns merely nodded. The taciturnity of the pathologist's laboratory assistant was legendary.

Detective Constable Crosby, who did not enjoy attending post-mortem examinations, positioned himself as far away as he could from the figure on the metal slab. Detective Inspector Sloan took up a stance at what he regarded as a decent distance and studied the dead woman carefully from there.

'Everything's ready for you now, Doctor,' murmured Burns, mercifully unspecific as to detail.

'We have here', Dr Dabbe began speaking into a microphone suspended above the examination table, 'the body of a young woman aged . . .' The pathologist looked across at the Detective Inspector. 'Do we know how old she was, Sloan? No sense in guessing if we know.'

'The husband says she was twenty-five,' replied Sloan carefully. The Superintendent would never accept an unsupported statement from Sloan or anyone else. As far as he was concerned, it was always hearsay until proved otherwise.

'Twenty-five . . . and the body has, I am informed,' said Dr Dabbe, resuming his reporting mode of speech into the microphone, 'been identified by the said husband as that of Mrs Margaret Collins.'

'Turned a nasty shade of grey when he said it was her, David Collins did,' put in Detective Constable Crosby gratuitously from the sidelines. 'He went nearly as pale as she is now when we showed her to him.'

'I thought he was going to flop on us,' admitted Detective Inspector Sloan. 'People do, of course.' That was when the police had to watch very carefully. There were those who thought that a genuine faint could easily be copied by the conscious, but it couldn't always.

'He was sweating, too,' added Crosby. It was one of the things he'd been taught to watch out for especially in anyone he was interviewing. 'They say you can't fake sweat.'

'Very true, but each to his own,' said Dr Dabbe, himself a man almost devoid of human reactions. 'The husband's your province, Constable, not mine.' The pathologist gave a wolfish grin. 'Remember, I only deal with the dead.'

'Quite so, Doctor,' put in Sloan. He often wished the same could be said of the police. The dead never attacked them.

'And I am advised that the deceased is thought to have been missing from half-past four yesterday afternoon,' continued Dr Dabbe, resuming his address to the microphone. He winked at his assistant. 'We like having a *terminus ab quo* and a *terminus ad quem*, don't we, Burns?'

'It helps, Doctor.'

'Gives us all something to go on,' agreed Detective Inspector Sloan. He had learned to be thankful for small police mercies . . .

'Saves a lot of work, too, if she was reported missing early on,' said Dr Dabbe.

'Not all that early on, Doctor,' said Sloan. 'Not until the middle of this morning, actually. By the husband, though.' If, thought Sloan irreverently to himself, the pathologist had been about to perform the legendary magician's act of sawing a woman in half on stage, he could hardly have set the scene better, even to the microphone suspended above the post-mortem table into which he was speaking now.

'Slightly built, well groomed and somewhat underweight for her height.' Dr Dabbe grinned and turned away from the microphone in an aside. 'We don't get many underweight women here, Inspector, unless they're anorexics or addicts – on the contrary, in fact. That right, Burns?'

'Yes, Doctor,' responded Burns dutifully.

'For heavyweight you can often read deadweight,' said the doctor pithily.

'Make a good slogan for slimming food, that would,' said Crosby from the sidelines, grateful for any diversion.

'Adequately nourished, though, all the same,' pronounced the pathologist, carrying on considering the dead woman's contours with the calculating eye of a sculptor. 'Rather a shapely figure, I should say. Good ankles and all that.' He jerked his head towards the microphone in an aside to an unknown secretary. 'Don't put that in the report, Beryl.'

Sloan registered this and nodded, his mind

107

wandering away again. He was actually wondering how accurately he could have described his own wife had it been she who had been missing. For one thing, he would have to state from the first that she, too, was well nourished. Mrs Sloan, there was no denying it, favoured Chaucer's Prioress in being 'by no means undergrown'.

'No signs of recent dieting visible on the skin,' Dr Dabbe was noting into the microphone again. 'And no macroscopic evidence of gross injury.'

'We know the deceased had been very anxious and worried lately about her son, who had had to have a serious operation,' offered Sloan. 'Comfortable' would have been how he would have had to describe his own wife's figure, although she wouldn't have wanted him to say anything about love handles, for sure: would have been very cross if he had . . . but not if she was dead and they needed to know why. It might be important then. Death changed things. This woman – Margaret Collins – wouldn't – couldn't – possibly mind how she was described. Not now . . .

The pathologist was looking carefully at the deceased's fingernails. 'Manicured and not broken,' he said, taking samples of scrapings from under the nails. He stepped back and scrutinized the whole body. 'In fact, no external signs of injury at all except to the face—'

'Ah, the face,' said Sloan. He'd noticed the blood on the woman's face himself while she was still in the maze.

'A bruised nose and some post-mortem bleeding,' said Dabbe. 'See how the blood hasn't travelled far?' He bent forward. 'Distribution consistent with the deceased having fallen forward face downwards on a hard surface after death—'

'Stone,' supplied Crosby.

'On which, as you saw, she was spreadeagled somewhat artistically,' Sloan reminded the pathologist.

'In front of the Minotaur himself,' said Dr Dabbe. 'Saw please, Burns.'

Crosby shut his eyes.

'Thank you.' The pathologist took the surgical saw and started to work away at the deceased's cranium. 'There's a divinity, Sloan, that shapes our ends, rough-hew them how we will.'

'Yes, Doctor,' said Sloan, agreeing with the general principle, even if some magistrates weren't so sure. They still believed that defendants had been masters of their own fates since birth.

'Some suicidal women take a lot of care about how they're going to look when they're found, you know.'

'Yes, Doctor.' That was something Sloan was aware of. The doctrine of free will was less certain. It was all very well for the courts to assign all the responsibility to the individual, but it wasn't like that in real life.

'Do anything for effect, if they have a mind to it, the ladies,' went on Dr Dabbe mordantly. 'If they've taken an overdose, that is, of course.'

'Pride is sometimes one of the last of the seven

109

deadly sins to go,' observed Detective Inspector Sloan, trying to remember something in a moralistic play which his church-going mother had made him read when young. Pride hadn't featured at all at Everyman's end, though, now he came to think of it. Everyman, poor fellow, on his way to the tomb had gradually lost all that made life worthwhile – Good Fellowship had gone early and his Five Wits, too. Only his Good Deeds had stayed with him to the last. He said this to Dr Dabbe, while Detective Constable Crosby opened his eyes and then averted them.

'Dante, you know, didn't even list Pride in his Circles of Hell,' remarked Dabbe. 'Though lust and gluttony were there.'

'More harmful than pride, perhaps,' said Sloan moderately. Gluttony didn't give them a lot of grief down at the police station, but the same certainly couldn't always be said for lust . . .

'Dante did have a Circle of Hell for those who were violent against the self,' remarked Dabbe as he continued his examination, 'if that's what's in your minds today, gentlemen.'

'We have nothing in our minds at the moment, Doctor,' promised Sloan. 'Not until you put it there.'

'You're as bad as the surgeons,' grinned Dabbe. 'They don't know what they're dealing with either until we've told 'em. That right, Burns?'

'Yes, Doctor,' said Burns.

The pathologist turned his attention from the skull to the alimentary canal. 'Surely you've heard the one about the physician, the psychiatrist, the surgeon and the pathologist, Inspector?'

'No, Doctor.' Category jokes were now out at the police station.

'Well, they were all out duck-shooting together and when one flew over, the physician spent so much time debating what tests he should do to make sure that it was a duck that he lost it . . . Spencer-Wells, please, Burns . . . thank you. When the next duck came over the psychiatrist wasn't sure that it was a duck and not repressed anxiety over whether his mother had loved him enough . . .' He stopped and peered down intently at something in the cadaver that had caught his eye. 'Retractor, please, Burns, while I take a look at the liver.'

'Out for a duck,' said Crosby.

'What's that, Constable?' said the doctor. 'Where was I?'

'Shooting ducks,' said Crosby.

'Oh, yes. Then another duck appeared. The surgeon shot it and turned to the pathologist and asked what it was.'

'I don't see . . .', began Crosby.

But the whole atmosphere in the mortuary changed suddenly as Dr Dabbe stooped further over. 'I think we may have found the cause of death, Sloan – can't be sure, of course, until we've done some more tests – but I should say that some noxious substance had been ingested.'

'Ah,' said Detective Inspector Sloan, glad he'd

instituted a search of the maze for a drinking vessel of any sort at all.

'Can't tell you what it was yet, Sloan, but the good news from our point of view is that there's some of it left in the stomach contents.'

'Which should help,' said Detective Constable Crosby, getting ready to go.

The pathologist shrugged. 'Not all that much, I'm afraid. The noxious substance – if that's what it was – may have killed her, but I reckon someone moved her after she'd had it.' His tone hardened. 'And they either banged her face on the stone as they arranged her there or her head fell forwards accidentally.' He straightened up. 'If that's what happened then you could be dealing with murder dressed up as suicide . . .' He grinned. 'Nearly as unattractive as mutton dressed as lamb, eh, gentlemen?'

Chapter Eleven

It was difficult to know who was the more upset in the Close at Calleford, the Bishop or his wife.

'You did what?' exploded Bertram Wallingford on a rising note, his much advertised commitment to non-aggressive behaviour seriously at risk.

'Oh, Bertie, that poor man,' said Mary, a wife as skilled in deploying diversionary tactics as any other woman. 'I know that that young Constable couldn't tell us anything when he came for David Collins, but we all know what being asked to identify a body means, don't we?'

'You gave my favourite dressing gown to the goat?' thundered the Bishop, a man renowned on his diocesan committees for sticking to the matter in hand.

'Your only dressing gown,' pointed out his wife unapologetically. 'The police must have been fairly sure it was Margaret Collins, mustn't they, to have come here for her husband like that?'

'Has the goat eaten it all?' he asked, still undeflected.

'It was very hungry,' said Mary Wallingford. She

reverted to David Collins. 'As if having his son so ill wasn't enough . . .'

'Pelion upon Ossa,' agreed the Bishop, finding as he often did that the Greeks had a better phrase than he could conjure up. He sought for an equally suitable quotation from the Book of Job, but soon gave up. He found, as usual, even to think about Job depressing beyond measure and immediately turned back to his own troubles. 'I was very fond of that dressing gown, Mary . . .'

She sighed. 'That poor little family. I sometimes wonder, Bertie, if the good Lord knows what he's about.'

Bertram Wallingford took a deep breath and was about to launch into a carefully prepared piece, often delivered from his pulpit, about the ways of the Lord being truly mysterious as well as being hidden from the sight of mere mortals, but thought better of it and closed his mouth without saying anything.

'Apparently David thought his wife was staying at the hospital with little James, which was why he came over here and carried on working yesterday evening,' said Mary.

'I know Double Felix have got as much work as they can handle,' said the Bishop, momentarily diverted from his grievance. 'They're a clever pair. They say there's no one to touch them in Calleshire in their own speciality. Did you know that they can conjure up an image just from light?'

Mary Wallingford was not and never had been interested in the sciences. 'I wish now I'd spent more time with Margaret when I went into the nursery, but we all knew how worried she was and you can't just go on about an illness, can you?'

'No,' said the Bishop firmly. 'That only makes it worse.'

'I wonder what will happen to that poor little boy now? Margaret Collins has a mother somewhere, I know.'

'Then she'll cope,' said her husband confidently. 'In my experience grandmothers always do.'

She gave a little laugh. 'It's funny how a big trouble soon drives out a little one, isn't it? I'd almost forgotten about that dead rabbit and the pentagram.'

'I hadn't,' said the Bishop seriously. 'Whichever way you look at it, Mary, it means trouble.'

'Aye, Inspector,' agreed Dr Angus Browne without hesitation, 'I gave Margaret Collins a prescription for some sleeping tablets called Crespusculan . . . let me see now . . . it must have been a month or more ago.'

'If we could just have the date, please, doctor . . .' said Sloan. In his experience, coroners liked firm figures of whatever nature.

'It was the night before the infant's first operation,' said the general practitioner, handing over a scribbled note on which was spelled the name of the sedative. 'I can tell you that.'

115

'Understandable,' said Sloan.

The doctor peered at the two policemen over the top of his spectacles. 'Mrs Collins would no' be reassured that the operation itself presented no danger to her son James.'

That was quite understandable in Sloan's view if not that of the medical profession, but he did not say so.

Dr Browne sighed. 'Besides, both husband and wife had stopped sleeping since the child's condition was diagnosed.'

'I'm not surprised,' said Crosby stoutly.

'Mercifully, it's a rare condition,' said the doctor.

'And the quantity of these tablets?' asked Sloan. Someone would have to be detailed to search the Collinses' house for any that might be left. Somehow he didn't think there would be many.

'Aye,' said the doctor. 'I take your point. He glanced down at his notes. 'Enough, I suppose, to do her a serious injury if she took the lot. I didn't think that likely, of course.'

'Why not?' asked Crosby.

The general practitioner turned to him. 'When a child is ill, Constable, motherhood usually triumphs over a depression, however deep.'

Detective Inspector Sloan nodded his agreement. 'Especially when their infant's at real risk, which seems to have been the case here.'

'Mind you, gentlemen, the child's illness was no' the only thing the parents had to worry about.'

116

Detective Inspector Sloan's head came up in a purely police reflex. 'No?'

'There was the question of the risk of further children suffering from the same condition. Not high, but sufficiently quantifiable – in statistical terms, that is – for David and Margaret Collins to have taken some action that might or might not have been strictly indicated to be on the safe side.'

What came into Sloan's mind while the doctor was going through these circumlocutions about sterilization was a mock sword slipping in a mock fight on stage in a school play. One of the combatants had gasped, 'Alas, I am unmanned,' and the whole class had fallen about in unseemly laughter.

'Done, was he?' asked Detective Constable Crosby informally.

'Quite so,' said Dr Browne. 'Coming back to the point, I can tell you that, as a rule, it isn't the needed who take overdoses. In my experience it's those who fear themselves to be unwanted who tend to make away with themselves.'

Detective Inspector Sloan waited until he was back in the police car before he extended that thought. 'And it's those who are unwanted who tend to be made away with, Crosby. Let's go and see Milly Smithers next.'

*   *   *   *   *

'Sit yourselves down,' said Milly Smithers comfortably. 'Tea?'

'Please,' said Sloan, settling himself at the kitchen table of a cottage just outside the gardens of Aumerle Court. 'Only a few questions, that's if you've got a moment.'

'No hurry on my account,' said Milly Smithers, turning to the sideboard. 'I'm home for the afternoon. I give Miss Daphne her lunch early in the summer. Then she can have a little nap before the visitors come in, while I come home and get on.'

'I gather she likes to keep her eye on them,' said Sloan, grateful for the steaming mug of tea she had put in front of him. At this stage he didn't know whether Miss Pedlinge qualified as a good witness of what went on in the maze or not. She just might have been someone who was thought to be a reliable witness but actually, like the child in Kipling's poem, had been well advised to 'Watch the wall, my darling, while the gentlemen go by'. Given sufficient motive, she would have been good at that, he thought.

'Gives her something to do, poor dear,' said Milly, sawing away at a large loaf. 'She gets a bit bored, sitting there all day in that wheelchair.'

'I don't wonder,' said Crosby, who was still young enough to think stillness synonymous with death.

Milly Smithers plonked a plate of ham on the table, pushed an opened packet of butter alongside it, and followed it with a breadboard on which stood a pile of roughly sliced bread. She invited the two policemen to help themselves. 'I go back in later to give her some supper and put her to bed. We have a coffee together and bit of a chat, then I tuck her up for the night and come home.'

'Last night no different?' asked Sloan, while Crosby eyed the ham.

'Same as usual,' said Milly. 'I left at about half-nine . . .'

'And locked up?'

'Like always,' she said without hesitation. 'I've got the key to the back gate. Saves me walking all the way round, for one thing. And I'm first back at the Court in the mornings, anyway, for all that Captain Prosser thinks he works the hardest.'

'You don't say?' murmured Sloan disingenuously.

She sniffed. 'You can't say that being in the Army doesn't do something for you because you've only got to remember that Miss Daphne was in it, too. But it doesn't seem to have taught him a lot.'

'Captain Prosser must have a key, too, surely?' said Sloan.

'I couldn't say, I'm sure,' said Milly Smithers. 'He doesn't communicate much.'

'And Mr Bevis?' Sloan introduced the name as he reached for a slice of bread, properly described as cut like a doorstep. 'Has he got a key?'

'I 'spect so,' said Milly. 'He only comes Sundays these days . . .'

'These days?'

'He used to bring his wife and children over at weekends, but they don't come any more.'

'Fallen out with Miss Daphne?'

'Fallen out with each other,' said the carer. 'That's what's worrying Miss Daphne.'

'Oh, dear,' said Sloan in as neutral a tone as he could muster.

'You may say, "Oh, dear," like that,' responded Millie Smithers strenuously, 'but it's important where somewhere like the Court is concerned. A big divorce settlement could upset Miss Daphne's plans.'

'I see.' He thought he could, too. 'And it's on the cards, is it?'

Milly sniffed. 'Seems that his wife thinks that some woman who's no better than she ought to be has been throwing herself at Mr Bevis—'

'And Mrs Pedlinge doesn't like it?'

'Well, would you?' asked the woman forthrightly. 'Mind you, he's a good-looking man, I will say that for him. Very. And charming with it. Always was since he was a boy, but he's got a wife and children to think of now—'

'And great expectations,' said Sloan, policeman first, last, and all the time.

'It's not his expectations that would be the problem,' Milly Smithers came back smartly. 'It would be his wife's.'

'How come?' asked Crosby, his mouth full.

'In the event of a divorce . . .'

'I see,' said Detective Inspector Sloan, doing a rapid

mental review of who was known to have been at Aumerle Court the day before with something on their mind. The field seemed to be widening.

'Could upset the applecart, that, couldn't it?' observed Detective Constable Crosby, turning to Milly. 'Would you happen to have any mustard handy?'

'So he should be being careful with Miss Daphne as well,' said Milly, 'instead of going ahead with this sound and light performance that he's written and he wants to put on and she doesn't.' Milly Smithers grimaced as she put the mustard jar on the table. 'Fancies himself as a bit of a playwright does our Mr Bevis, and the Captain's no better. The pair of them are in it together, no matter what Miss Daphne says.'

'She doesn't think they are?' said Sloan, thinking quickly. An unholy alliance between the heir and the agent could lead anywhere. Anywhere at all. And cover anything up, too.

'He's a dark horse is the Captain,' said Milly obliquely. 'And Miss Daphne forgets that Mr Bevis wanted him to have the job pretty badly. Spoke up for him in a big way when he got the shove from the Ornums, Mr Bevis did, I heard.'

'He did, did he?' Sloan made another mental note and included in it the fact that Milly Smithers seemed to hear most things. Someone would have to check out exactly why Captain Prosser had lost his job.

'Mr Bevis and the Captain are neighbours over at Nether Hoystings,' said Milly. 'I expect that's why.'

'This sound and light play . . .'

'The Captain thinks something like that'll boost visitor numbers, but does he say so to Miss Daphne?'

'No?' said Sloan, watching Crosby pile ham on to bread and butter as if famine loomed.

'No, he doesn't. It's all "Yes, Miss Pedlinge" and "No, Miss Pedlinge",' she said. 'Not that it washes with her. She may be old but she's not silly yet.'

'Perhaps he's just diplomatic,' said Sloan.

'Deceitful,' countered Milly. 'But, take it from me, all the Captain thinks about is visitor numbers and leaning on the staff.' She turned to Crosby. 'I gotta nice jar of pickle, young man, if you fancy that. Made it myself.'

'It's very good ham,' the Constable said appreciatively.

'I cook it myself,' she said, pleased. 'I take a bit in for Miss Daphne's supper from time to time. She likes it, too.'

But the ready provision to members of the constabulary of home-cooked ham and pickle and lashings of tea did not automatically eliminate witnesses from police enquiries: especially when those witnesses held keys to gates and were spear-carriers for other important witnesses. Detective Inspector Sloan reminded himself to make this quite clear to Detective Constable Crosby on their way back to the police station at Berebury.

And that the fact that Bevis Pedlinge clearly came of a good family had no bearing on the matter either.

Cain had belonged to a good family, too.

Chapter Twelve

'We wanted to interview Captain Prosser as well, sir,' explained Detective Inspector Sloan to Superintendent Leeyes back at the police station, 'but we were told he had gone over to Calleford to talk to his solicitor.'

Leeyes brightened immediately. 'That's a hopeful sign, Sloan. Innocent men don't need solicitors to advise them to keep their mouths shut.'

This was not everybody's view, but all Sloan said was that they were also waiting to talk to Mr Bevis Pedlinge and would do so as soon as his train from London arrived at Calleford station. 'He, David Collins and Captain Prosser, sir, were all in the maze yesterday afternoon.'

'And is it to be a case of "Eenie, meanie, miney, mo"?' enquired the Superintendent acidly, 'or have you got a favourite in the murder stakes – if it is murder?'

'Not yet, sir,' said Sloan, manfully refraining from making a retort based roughly on the principle of it being at this stage more of a case of 'you pays your

money and takes your choice'. He hastened on. 'I have
had a message from the SOCO stating that a poly-
styrene cup has been found stuffed in the yew hedge
not far from the deceased.' He had given full marks to
the scene of crime officer for spotting it so quickly,
keeping to himself the unworthy thought that she
might have been meant to do just that by the person
who had placed it so that it would be found – but not
too easily.

'Ah . . .'

'It's gone over to forensic to see what can be made
of the dregs.'

'Not drained to the last drop, then, Sloan, eh?' He
grimaced. 'My middle name isn't Patsy, you know.'

'No, sir – I mean, yes, sir.' There was no denying
that, despite all his idiosyncrasies, Superintendent
Leeyes still had an eye for essentials. 'It had been
placed in the hedge the right way up.'

'Someone trying to make fools of us, do you think?'
He scowled.

'Could be,' admitted Sloan. He didn't know yet, but
he would find out. In due course. He didn't like the
idea of being anyone's patsy any more than did the
Superintendent.

'Can't be having that,' said the Superintendent
combatively.

'Forensic are doing an analysis of the liquid left in
the cup for us as a matter of priority, sir. Then it can be
compared with the stomach contents and the sedative
prescribed by the deceased's doctor.'

'Any of that left at the bedside by any remote chance or am I being cynical?'

'Not even a bottle, sir.'

David Collins had willingly acceded to a police request to go round his house. He had left them to it, sitting in the kitchen by himself, his head sunk in his hands, while Sloan and Crosby had examined the Collinses' matrimonial bedroom.

'With the intention that we look for it, do you suppose?' growled Leeyes.

'Could be,' Sloan said again. 'We're still searching the maze and I've got more men going over the house now. And a woman.'

'Women sometimes notice things a man wouldn't,' conceded the Superintendent unexpectedly. It was rumoured at the police station that the Superintendent's wife noticed everything. And forgave nothing.

'And', plodded on his subordinate, 'forensic are taking a very good look at the soles of the deceased's sandals . . .'

'For signs of gravel from the maze, I take it?' grunted Leeyes. 'And from anywhere else, of course. The hospital car park, for instance . . .'

'For any indication that any gravel in the sandals was pressed into the soles other than by someone of the weight of the deceased, sir.' Detective Inspector Sloan didn't like having the wool pulled over his eyes any more than did the next man – the next policeman, anyway – and he wasn't going to let it happen now if he could help it.

'I think I get your drift,' grunted Leeyes, scribbling something on a piece of paper on his desk. He gave a cynical chuckle. 'Did she walk or was she pushed? That's it, isn't it? Anything else?'

'Forensic are examining both the big industrial dustbins on site, too—'

'Inside and out, I hope, Sloan.'

'Yes, sir,' he sighed, 'although probably any deeper marks than usual made by their wheels have been lost by now.'

'On the supposition that that was how the body reached the centre of the maze?'

'It's one option we're exploring.' He hesitated. 'There are a number of others.'

The Superintendent said, 'Go on.'

'It's the time-frame that's so interesting.' Sloan squinted down at his notebook. 'Miss Pedlinge checked as usual—'

'That's the old bird with everything still on a war footing, isn't it?' interrupted Leeyes.

'Yes, sir.' He began again. 'Miss Pedlinge checked,' he stopped at once and corrected himself. He couldn't – shouldn't take anything about that old lady for granted – especially if her great-nephew could be in the frame. 'Or, rather, Miss Pedlinge says that she checked as usual that there was no one in the maze and gave the signal to the gate at half-past five so that they could lock up and go. That gate had been closed to all newcomers at half-past four as usual.'

'And the back gate?' pounced Leeyes.

'Closed to vehicles at five o'clock and to pedestrians just before half-past nine by the carer, Milly Smithers, as she always did.'

'And it was dark when?'

'Just after seven, sir.'

The Superintendent leaned back in his chair. 'So either this Margaret Collins walked in after dark and found her way to the bull in the middle . . .' He stopped. 'Do you suppose, Sloan, that's why the centre of a target is called the bull's eye?'

'I couldn't say, I'm sure, sir.' Detective Inspector Sloan's personal interaction with Greek myths and legends had been limited to removing young men and maidens from Berebury's own statue of Eros every May Day.

'Either, then, Sloan,' he pronounced hortatively, 'the deceased got there under her own steam without being spotted or somebody got to the same place with her body in a bin.'

'But both in the dark.' As far as Sloan was concerned that went for him, too. 'And, according to Dr Dabbe, her face was slightly injured after death, probably when her head fell forward on the stone.'

'Which it wouldn't have done,' pronounced the Superintendent ineluctably, 'if she had lain down carefully herself.'

'That, sir,' sighed Sloan, 'is exactly how far we've got at the moment.'

Waving him away with a hand, the Superintendent said loftily, 'Then, Sloan, it's what the psychologists describe as "a problem in resolution". Let me know how you get on.'

Mrs Amanda Pedlinge waved Detective Inspector Sloan and Detective Constable Crosby into a pair of chairs which both looked uncomfortable and were. The address of the family – the Old Rectory at Nether Hoystings – was about the only thing in the room that could be described as other than very up to date. Everything else in sight about the place was ultra-modern and minimalist. Unfortunately, decided Sloan, lowering himself carefully on to one, that included the chairs.

And, to a policeman, it all spelled money.

'Well, and what's my husband been up to now?' she asked the policemen.

'Nothing, madam, as far as we know,' said Sloan. Mrs Pedlinge certainly fitted the decor well: tall, thin and dressed with a classic plainness that betokened a good eye for clothes – and how to wear them. He didn't mind about her being so stick thin, but he would have preferred the chairs to have been more substantial. 'We just need a little assistance with our enquiries, that's all.'

Amanda Pedlinge pushed some strands of ash-blonde hair away from her eyes and arranged herself carefully on another chair, crossing one elegant leg over the other. 'That's what they always say, isn't it, Inspector?'

CATHERINE AIRD

'Only in bad films,' said Detective Constable Crosby before Sloan could speak.

'What we would like to know is where Mr Pedlinge was yesterday evening,' said Sloan, deciding circumlocution would not be the right approach with this manifestly disgruntled young woman, 'after he left Aumerle Court.'

'So would I,' Mrs Pedlinge said with some vigour.

'Ah.' Sloan began to wonder if she might be as uncomfortable to live with as one of her chairs.

'Dinner was quite spoilt by the time he came home,' she said petulantly. 'And I'd put the children to bed early so that we could have a good long talk.'

'So he wasn't here?' said Sloan, leaving aside for the time being the question of what the talk might have been going to be about.

'He most certainly was not,' said Mrs Pedlinge. 'And if he says he was, then he's lying.'

'That means you were here yourself, then, I take it,' said Sloan smoothly.

The ash-blonde hair shook with indignation. 'I'm here all the time,' she said. 'That's the trouble. It's London and work all week and Aumerle Court with that old armchair warrior every Sunday for him and nothing for me any of the time except small children and you know what that's like.'

'There's Satur—' began Crosby, who hadn't taken his eyes off the pair of long legs waving ever so gently in front of him and who had no concept of the trials and tribulations of being corralled with small children.

'And where do you suppose he was yesterday evening then, madam?' asked Sloan quickly, trying hard to project sympathy with matrimonial absences. Crosby was so mesmerized by a foot from which a fashionable shoe was now dangling that – unlike Bevis Pedlinge – he would probably have to be prised away from the house.

'Don't ask me, Inspector,' she snapped, the movement of the loose shoe taking on a new rhythm. 'Ask him.'

'I will, madam, I will.' Perhaps 'shoe' was too strong a word for the stylish leather contrivance that was swinging from Amanda Pedlinge's shapely ankle: he decided that 'foot ornament' described it better.

'And when you get an answer from him – if you do – tell me and I'll tell my solicitors.'

'You have reason to suppose that this would be of interest to them?' Detective Inspector Sloan automatically registered the fact that she spoke of her solicitors in the plural. People who did that usually referred to their bankers in the plural, too, and that meant money.

'Oh, yes, Inspector,' she said with a shrill laugh, 'they'll be interested all right and so will I.'

'But you yourself have no suggestions to make as to his whereabouts?' he asked patiently. 'He didn't tell you?'

'Me?' she laughed again. 'He doesn't tell me anything, Inspector. It's always the same story – that it's just business that's keeping him wherever he is and when – and if it's not that, then it's this wretched production that they're putting on at Aumerle Court.'

'Tell me more . . .'

She needed no encouragement. 'The history of the Pedlinge family in sound and light. You know, they throw pictures all over the place with laser beams and record the dialogue to go with it. We've got a neighbour who's into that sort of thing professionally – David Collins of Double Felix. Jeremy Prosser put Bevis on to him.' She sighed. 'He's very good at his job and he knows what he's doing, but the others are nothing more than schoolboys playing at amateur dramatics, really. The lot of them . . .'

The implication that Amanda Pedlinge was rather more than a schoolgirl was not lost upon Detective Inspector Sloan, married man. He couldn't answer for the goggle-eyed Detective Constable Crosby.

'Bevis has written the script and it's about the only thing he talks about these days.' She waved a hand. 'I expect he'll say he was doing something with the sound or the light.'

Somewhere from the back of Sloan's mind something about 'sound and fury signifying nothing' surfaced, but he didn't immediately track it down.

'We got Collins to do this room,' she said, looking round at a room seemingly without electrical fitments of any sort.

'Very clever, madam. I can't see where any of it is coming from.'

Amanda Pedlinge looked pleased for the first time.

'There's not meant to be anything in sight at all with this sort of interior design. David Collins made an excellent job of that. Even Bevis was satisfied.' At this point her shoe fell off her right foot and on to the floor in front of Detective Constable Crosby. 'For once.'

'Where to now, sir?' asked Detective Constable Crosby as they crunched across the drive of the Old Rectory and into their police car.

'Another word with the husband wouldn't come amiss,' said Sloan, reaching for the car radio. 'He only lives round the corner and anyway our other two runners aren't around to interview yet.'

'But he told us he was over at the Minster yesterday evening,' said Crosby. 'Working.'

'I didn't say he was the favourite,' said Sloan mildly. 'Just a runner. All three of 'em had been in the maze yesterday afternoon, remember.'

'The deceased must have reached the centre of the maze after dark,' objected Crosby, 'if the old lady says so.'

'And in the dark, too,' murmured Sloan. Authoritative old ladies had to be checked out, too. All in good time, of course.

'That old bird at the window could have spotted her, sir, at any time in daylight,' said the Constable, not paying attention.

'True, and their being there might have nothing to do with the death,' allowed Sloan. He wasn't here to teach Crosby logic; he was on duty trying to establish whether an unhappy woman had died at the hand of herself or another.

'Also-rans?' The Constable had just had to effect the arrest of a bookie and it had opened his eyes to the Turf and its lingo.

'Perhaps. Don't forget, too, Crosby, that the deceased must have been in there, or at least in the grounds, before our Milly locked the postern gate for the night.'

'Anyway,' nodded Crosby, 'the doctor said she would have been dead by then.'

'The place is pretty secure otherwise,' said Sloan, pursuing another line of thought which had just struck him. 'The people who built Aumerle Court didn't want to be taken by surprise by their enemies and they made sure that they weren't.' He was old enough to know that all God's children had enemies: what he didn't know yet was who had been Margaret Collins's enemy . . . Or even for sure if it had been herself. A lot of people were their own worst enemies . . .

'All the same, sir,' insisted the Constable obstinately, 'Calleford's quite a way away.'

'Dangerous things, amateur dramatics,' said Sloan elliptically, as he raised an answer on the radio from headquarters. 'DI Sloan here,' he announced. 'I would like a thorough search made of the area round the hospital car park for an empty tablet bottle – and if there's no joy from that, then impound the hospital bins and get someone to start going through them . . .

yes, thank you, I do know all about needles in haystacks. Over and out and get on with it.'

The Constable looked quite mystified. 'Amateur dramatics, sir?'

'It's just possible that in the course of setting up this entertainment Master Bevis Pedlinge might have been seeing a bit too much of Margaret Collins for her own good. Or his, come to that.'

'Enough to kill her?'

'Enough for someone to arrange for her to be killed,' said Sloan. 'What do you suppose it would do to the Aumerle estate if that blonde bombshell we've just left had to be paid off?' He supposed that there had been men thoroughly upset by the Married Women's Property Act: what they would have thought of today's divorce settlements didn't bear thinking about.

'I hadn't thought of divorce, sir,' said the Detective Constable.

'Neither had I until just now,' said Detective Inspector Sloan honestly, 'but some people think about it all the time.'

'She's quite a girl . . .'

'Remember, in this job, Crosby,' he said severely, 'nothing should be taken for granted. Nothing at all.'

'No, sir.'

'Nor forgotten. Such as the fact that Jeremy Prosser is a neighbour, too. If I were to draw a Venn diagram' – the Superintendent had explained to all of 'F' Division exactly how to draw overlapping circles demonstrating who is known to whom one morning after he

135

had attended an evening class on 'Mathematics for the Barely Numerate' – 'then Jeremy Prosser, Bevis and Amanda Pedlinge and David and Margaret Collins would all show as knowing each other.' He paused. 'No, we don't know yet that Amanda Pedlinge and Margaret Collins had met. It's probable, though.'

'Miss Daphne Pedlinge knows 'em all, too, sir,' volunteered Crosby.

'No,' Sloan corrected him. 'She didn't recognize the deceased – not from what she could see, anyway.'

'But they all knew the maze,' said Detective Constable Crosby, engaging gear. 'Didn't they?'

Chapter Thirteen

David Collins treated the second visit to his house by the police that day with a tired disinterest. A half-drunk mug of coffee stood, cold now, on the table in front of him. The man might not have moved since they had come to the house earlier, so still was he sitting when they came again. All that was different was that now his shirt was open and his sleeves were hanging loose and dishevelled.

'Margaret's mother should be here soon,' he said, pushing the mug away as if the action took all his strength. 'Then we'll have to go to the hospital and collect poor James and—'. For a moment he seemed to be having trouble finishing the sentence. 'And', he resumed, collecting himself with a visible effort, 'she's going to tell him that his mummy's . . . I'm sorry.' His voice quavered and his narrative came to a shaky halt. 'It's no good.' He sank his head back between his hands. 'I can't quite take it in yet that Margaret's gone.'

'It's very difficult, I know,' said Detective Inspector Sloan with a brisk sympathy, 'but you'll understand that we need to know everything that happened yesterday for the Coroner.' Over the years Sloan had found that mention of this august official usually evoked a more ready compliance with questioning than did any amount of talk of police interviews.

Collins raised his head. 'Go on,' he said bleakly.

'Just for the record, sir, can we take it that as far as you know your wife had no enemies?'

'None. Not Margaret.'

'Then could we just go over again what happened from when you left your wife at the hospital?'

He didn't seem to mind. 'I went over to Aumerle Court, like I said, to meet Mr Bevis Pedlinge and Captain Prosser over this great sound and light production they've got planned.'

'You knew them before yesterday?'

'Oh, yes. They both live out here in this village. I've done quite a lot of work for the Pedlinges one way and another and Jeremy Prosser's quite a family friend these days . . .' he stopped suddenly, a stricken look coming over his face. 'Only we're not going to be a family any more, are we?'

'Tell me about Captain Prosser,' said Sloan, interested. If David Collins liked him, he would seem to be the only person he'd met so far who did.

The man smiled faintly. 'I can tell you that he's not quite the stuffy bachelor he'd like you to think. In fact, I'm told in the village that he's something of a ladies' man.'

'Ah.' So someone liked Jeremy Prosser after all. And if Bevis Pedlinge wasn't the happily married man he'd presumably like everyone, but especially his Great-aunt Daphne, to think, then interviewing the pair of them might be a rewarding business. 'And then?' he asked Collins.

'We all went into the maze and I took some measurements away with me – I told them that we'll have to do quite a lot of calculations back at the office before we can start over there with the actual equipment. Throwing light up from the maze and then playing about with it is going to be quite a tricky job – we'll need plenty of thyristors for a start.'

'And after that?' said Sloan. Learning what thyristors were would have to wait.

'I left just before they shut up shop at the Court and took myself over to the Minster at Calleford.'

'Straight there?'

He shook his head. 'I stopped the van in a layby outside Petering for a cuppa.' He essayed a tired smile. 'I suppose I could have waited until I got to the Minster, but I didn't like to have a drink there. The place is plastered with notices about the ungodly not eating and drinking in the Close.'

'And?'

'And then I went on to Calleford and started work there.' He said diffidently, 'You – the police, I mean – may not have heard about it over in Berebury, but they've been having trouble with intruders in the Minster Close and Double Felix – that's our firm – has been asked to put in extra security lighting in some dark corners as quickly as poss.'

'Plenty of dark corners there,' contributed Crosby.

'I'll say,' Collins agreed warmly. 'It's quite creepy in the Close after dark, I can tell you, but as I say they wanted the work doing like yesterday.'

'See anyone?' asked Sloan casually.

'The men on the gate – oh, and the Dean and the Bishop went by after Evensong. They were going over to the Bishop's Palace.'

'And they didn't say anything about six days shalt thou labour?' asked Detective Inspector Sloan, well-brought-up son of a church-going mother.

'They didn't speak to me at all,' responded Collins. 'They were talking to each other as they went by. I'm surprised, though, that they didn't stop outside Canon Shorthouse's house in the Close.'

'For why?' asked Detective Constable Crosby, already bored.

'There were some funny noises coming from his garden,' said Collins.

'Funny as in peculiar?' asked the Constable.

'Myself, I could have sworn it was a goat bleating,' said Collins with a light laugh, 'but then I decided I must be imagining things and got on with the job.'

'Which you finished when?' At this point in the investigation it wasn't easy to see where a goat called Aries came in. If it did. But Aries had gone missing at much the same time as Margaret Collins and, like Margaret Collins, it had gone missing between Berebury and Calleford. The goat, though, was still alive and well. It, too, would have to be followed up . . .

'I didn't quite finish the work,' said Collins, 'but I decided I'd had enough for one day. I reckoned I'd earned a drink and I thought I'd better pack up before they closed.' He lifted his hand with his first sign of animation. 'Don't worry, Inspector. I took the van home first and walked to our local at Nether Hoystings.'

'The Dog and Duck,' put in Crosby.

'And I didn't have a drink until I got there,' said David Collins firmly, 'and I walked home afterwards.'

'Very wise, sir,' said Detective Inspector Sloan. This man was obviously no different from the generality of the population in thinking that drinking and driving – or just driving – was the only activity that really engaged police attention. It wasn't, and he made a mental note to send Crosby to check on the appearance at the Dog and Duck of a tired pedestrian the night before.

Collins sunk his head down between his hands again and groaned. 'And all the time I thought Margaret was safe in the hospital with James.'

A favourite quotation of Sloan's mother was something about being safe in the arms of Jesus instead, but this didn't seem the moment to say so.

Detective Constable Crosby clearly experienced no such delicate feelings. 'And all the time she was dead,' he said egregiously.

* * * * *

'There was undoubtedly a goat in Canon Shorthouse's garden, Inspector,' the Bishop of Calleford assured him. 'I'm afraid how it got there, though, is a complete mystery to us all.'

'And why,' chimed in the Clerk of Works defensively. Barry Wright was accustomed to taking the blame for all material defects in the Minster and Close and thought the presence of the goat might well be considered one of them.

'The Canon is, as it happens, the "Deliverance from Evil" specialist for the diocese in the matter of exorcisms and so forth,' the Bishop informed them, 'although he is presently away.'

Detective Constable Crosby gave a strangled snort. 'I thought that was what we did down at the station,' he said under his breath. 'Delivered people from evil.'

'Which', continued the Bishop serenely, 'may be relevant.'

Barry Wright hastened to agree with this. Spiritual matters were not included in his remit.

'And the goat has always had – er – an especial significance historically with evil,' went on the Bishop. 'It is usually associated with lust—'

'It was a billy goat,' put in Detective Constable Crosby from the sidelines, more audibly this time.

'A young British Alpine or goatling,' murmured the Bishop, 'so Alison Kirk from the Edsway Animal Sanctuary tells me.'

'There aren't any Alps in Britain . . .', began Crosby truculently.

'There were these other things, too, beside the goat,' said Barry Wright, still anxious to pass the buck. 'Bones and diagrams on doorsteps.' In his opinion, the reluctance of ordained clergy to call things by their proper names led to a lot of confusion. He'd always thought proper words in proper places were what education was all about.

'The pentagram was outside my own door, Inspector,' said the Bishop, 'and it's just as symbolic in its way as the dead animal I found there, too.'

'When was the goat put in the Canon's garden?' asked Detective Inspector Sloan, sticking firmly to the mundane.

'Ah, there you have me, Inspector,' admitted the Bishop. 'Perhaps our Clerk of Works here can help.'

'He can't,' said Barry Wright flatly, 'and neither can Security.' Personally he doubted whether Security would have noticed a herd of elephants tramping through the Close after the night shift came on and, lazy beggars that they were, he didn't for one moment suppose that they would have done anything about it if they had. 'All I can say is that there's no question of the goat having strayed into Canon Shorthouse's garden. It was tethered to a tree.'

'And hungry,' said the Right Reverend Bertram Wallingford a trifle plaintively.

In his time Detective Inspector Sloan had of necessity become acquainted with an array of recondite subjects. The feeding pattern of goats was not one of them.

Yet.

'David Collins tells me he heard the goat bleating', he said to Bertram Wallingford, 'and that you passed him in the early evening.'

'Indeed we did, Inspector. The Dean and I saw him working over by the slype as we came out of the Minster after Evensong and went over to my house for supper.'

'And how long have these – er – odd articles been appearing in the Close?' asked Sloan.

The Bishop and the Clerk of Works exchanged glances. 'About a week,' said the Bishop.

Barry Wright nodded in agreement. 'The first lot were there last Monday morning,' he said. 'That's when we called in Double Felix.'

'Why them?' asked Sloan. The firm of Double Felix seemed to pop up everywhere.

'They're quite well known in their line of business,' the Clerk of Works informed him. 'That's why we get them in.'

'They did the lighting for the Minster nativity play,' said the Bishop at the same moment.

'And repaired it when the donkey knocked over the crib and fused the lot,' said Barry Wright, who had had to beat off a spirited attempt by the play's producer to charge the work to the Clerk of Works' maintenance budget.

'Tell me, Inspector,' said the Bishop, 'do you hold out any hope of being able to catch the perpetrators of these desecrations in the Close?'

Detective Inspector Sloan, who thought he had a more serious crime on his hands than desecration, fell back on a time-honoured response. 'Too soon to say, I'm afraid, your Grace. Much too soon.'

Chapter Fourteen

In the nature of things members of the police force are more often the harbingers of bad news than good. The lady at Pear Tree Farm – Mrs Penelope Fellowes – therefore welcomed Detective Constable Crosby with a controlled wariness. He had found her in a field behind the farm, leading a handful of young male goats out to their paddock.

'Hello, there,' she called out when she spotted him arriving. 'I'm over here if you want me.'

Crosby advanced with a certain amount of caution towards a middle-aged woman dressed in a very odd assortment of clothes indeed.

'It's all right,' she reassured him, pointing to the goats. 'They're only young males. They don't do any harm,' she paused and amended this, 'except perhaps to young females – female goats, I mean. Goats mature early, you know.'

Crosby said he didn't know.

'Can't leave 'em together after ten weeks,' she said. 'They're precocious creatures, goats.' She shut the gate of the paddock and turned to face him.

'So what's the news then?'

'Your missing goat has been found,' he said. 'He's safe and well.'

'Thank God for that,' she said, visibly relieved. 'Where was he?'

'In the Minster Close at Calleford,' said Detective Constable Crosby.

Mrs Fellowes gave a hearty laugh. 'I suppose then I should say "Thank God" for that too, eh?'

'I couldn't say, I'm sure,' said the Constable seriously, 'though I understand the Bishop found it.'

'Good for him,' said Mrs Fellows. 'I must be sure to thank him. Very important, that. Wasn't it Rudyard Kipling who wrote, "Be polite but not friendly to Bishops"?'

'I couldn't say, I'm sure, madam.' All that Crosby knew about Kipling was that he had written a poem called 'If', which nobody he knew had ever been able to live up to.

'But how in heaven's name did Aries get there of all places?'

'I couldn't say, madam,' said Crosby truthfully. 'We wondered if you could tell us.'

'No,' said Mrs Fellowes frankly, shaking her head. 'I can't even begin to think why poor Aries should have been abducted, poor thing, let alone taken to Calleford.'

'When did you miss him, madam?' The Detective Constable got out his notebook in the approved style.

'Not until this morning. He was there all right with

147

the others when they all went back into their house for their afternoon feed yesterday and I'm pretty sure he was around when I gave the kids their evening bottles at half-past seven, although I couldn't swear to it . . .' She gave the Constable a curious look. 'Will there be anything to swear to, officer?'

'Too soon to say, madam,' he responded evasively.

'But he definitely wasn't there when I opened up this morning just after seven o'clock.'

'One goat looks very like another,' ventured Crosby unwisely. 'Could you have been mistaken?'

'No, Constable, I could not,' she came back frostily. 'You know your criminals and I know my goats.' She pushed a stray wisp of windswept hair back off her forehead. 'I had a good hunt for him after I'd done the milking and when I couldn't find him I rang my neighbours and asked them to have a look. And then I rang the police.'

'So,' said Crosby, 'he – Aries, I mean – could have gone—'

'Been taken,' she interrupted him swiftly.

'Been taken any time after half-past seven yesterday evening?'

'True. But why on earth should he have been? As goats go, he's not even especially valuable, although', she added loyally, 'he's a fine chap and I'm very fond of him.'

'There is some suggestion of black magic at the Minster, madam . . .'

Mrs Fellowes threw back her head and roared with

laughter. 'Oh, poor Aries . . . not that . . . he would be quite affronted at the very idea. My goats know I always think of them when I sing the Benedicite.'

'Beg pardon, madam?' Notebooks, Crosby decided, were all very well in their way, but not if you weren't quite sure what to write down in them. Or how to spell it.

Mrs Fellowes opened her mouth and sang in a surprisingly pure voice, '"O all ye Beasts and Cattle, bless ye the Lord: praise him and magnify him for ever."'

Detective Constable Crosby was on his way out through the gate before he remembered to turn round and call back, 'Aries is over at the Edsway Animal Sanctuary.' He hoped the goat lady had heard him, but he didn't stay to make sure.

If he had been being driven by anyone else, Detective Inspector Sloan would have used the travelling time between the police station and Aumerle Court for quiet cogitation. Quiet cogitation, alas, was never possible when Detective Constable Crosby was at the wheel.

'For reasons which do not concern us now, Crosby,' he said acidly, as the car caromed round a corner at what Sloan thought a quite unnecessary pace, 'it's only brides who need to be got to specific places on time. Not detectives engaged on a murder enquiry who could do with a little spare thinking time.'

'Not much to think about, though, is there, sir?' said Crosby, in no whit put out.

'I see. You've solved the case, have you?'

'The husband,' said the Constable simply.

'And may I ask why, since he seems to be the only person in sight with a cast-iron alibi for the hours of darkness before the postern gate was locked?'

'That's why,' said Crosby illogically.

'That's all very fine and large,' said Sloan trenchantly, 'but a little hard evidence wouldn't come amiss.' Nor, in his view, would another word with Miss Daphne Pedlinge, which was why they were heading for Aumerle Court now at a ridiculous speed.

'The Super is always saying that most murderers are widowers', said Crosby, putting his foot down practically to the floorboard, 'because they've killed their wives.'

'All right, then,' sighed Sloan, caught as ever between the unthinking and the unknowing, but not ignoring the Superintendent's mantra either, 'tell me how the husband did it. And why,' he added, although this didn't seem the moment to lecture Crosby on the legal irrelevance of motive, murder once being done.

'With mirrors, I expect,' grinned the Detective Constable, overtaking the startled rider of a Harley-Davidson motorcycle, a man not accustomed in the normal course of events to travelling behind other vehicles. 'As to why, I couldn't say, sir, not being married myself.'

The motorcyclist was not the only person to be

surprised that afternoon. In the Long Gallery, talking earnestly to Miss Daphne Pedlinge, was a thick-set young man with tow-coloured hair whom she introduced as 'M'great-nephew, Bevis.'

Detective Inspector Sloan advanced with interest. 'And we thought you were still in London . . .'

'I thought I'd better come down,' he said briefly.

'Ah,' Sloan nodded. The old lady had been quick off the mark, all right. 'A word with you, if we may, would be very helpful at this juncture, sir.'

He found himself being regarded with a calculating look by a man whose appearance was a faint echo of that of Miss Pedlinge with overtones of the rugby field. 'You, too, Inspector? I've just been grilled by my great-aunt.'

'Take no notice, Inspector,' snorted Daphne Ped-linge, all animation. 'Bevis here doesn't even know the meaning of the word. He'd have been no good under proper interrogation, I can tell you.'

'I say—' protested Bevis.

'Wouldn't have lasted five minutes without giving way,' pronounced the old lady. 'The young don't have any stamina these days.'

That was another of Superintendent Leeyes's mantras, too, but Sloan did not echo it now: in his experience what the young always did have was an ample supply of passion, if sometimes misguided. He wasn't sure, though, whether whoever had killed Mrs Margaret Collins had been exercising passion – cold-blooded calculation, more like. Getting her to take an

151

overdose, manoeuvring a comatose woman to the centre of the maze in the dark – after Miss Pedlinge had turned her attention to her tea, anyway – and making an unobserved withdrawal bespoke of much careful planning to him.

But passion could have come into the equation, too. So, it seemed to him, could Bevis and Amanda Pedlinge – that lady could well be playing for high stakes in the matter of a matrimonial settlement.

'So,' said Sloan, 'what exactly did Miss Pedlinge extract from you, sir, if I might ask?'

Bevis Pedlinge ran his hand through his hair and said ruefully, 'The fact that I was in the maze yesterday afternoon with Jeremy Prosser and David Collins, although I still don't see—'

'And was there any reason why you shouldn't have been?' enquired Sloan silkily. The possibility that any two – or even three – of the men had been acting in concert was something else that he mustn't overlook. A chant to do with the starting of horse races drifted unbidden into his mind. How did it go? 'One to make ready, And two to prepare; good luck to the rider and away goes the mare . . .' Had Margaret Collins been the mare?

'Not a reason exactly . . .' Bevis Pedlinge was squirming under his great-aunt's gaze.

'They were plotting against me,' said a voice from the wheelchair. 'All of them – to say nothing about acting against my express wishes.' She stopped and added with icy precision, 'Against my wishes clearly expressed, too.'

'But Aunt Daphne—'

'Aumerle Court isn't going to be turned into a theme park while I'm alive, Inspector . . .'

Detective Inspector Sloan had heard artificial arguments before – some staged entirely for his benefit. He waited until this one had been played out before him: this, after all, was not an official questioning under caution.

'But Aunt Daphne—'

'By my great-nephew or Captain Prosser, more gate money or not. I have told them before that that was my last word on the subject.' She twisted the wheelchair until she was staring out of the window again. 'Amateur dramatics with sound and light at Aumerle Court indeed! Whatever next?'

'Perhaps', Sloan invited him, 'you would care to tell us exactly what you did do in the maze.' His concern was with whoever had arranged the making 'away with the mare', not the takings of Aumerle Court.

'Help with the measuring up for the lighting,' said Bevis Pedlinge shortly. 'Since my aunt chooses to keep the plan of the maze under lock and key we had to do it all by hand, so to speak, so that Double Felix could get on with working out the circuits for the performance.'

'And after that?'

Bevis Pedlinge's face took on a dull red flush, which belied the casual way in which he said, 'I visited a friend in the hospital at Berebury and then I went home.'

153

'Which ward?'

'Not a ward,' he said thickly. 'A department. Accident and Emergency.' He rose to his feet. 'And that's where I'm going now, whatever anyone says. Good day to you all.'

The wheelchair reversed noiselessly back to face the room as he left. 'There now,' said Miss Daphne with satisfaction. 'What did I tell you, Inspector? He's no good under questioning. No good at all.'

'What I would really like to know, Miss Pedlinge,' said Sloan quietly, 'is how to go round the maze on my own.'

Her lips twitched. 'I thought you'd never ask, Inspector. It's easy. Go in and don't backtrack until you get to a dead end.'

'And then?' Hitting the buffers was all very well, but usually it didn't help.

'Then only come back as far as the next opening and take that.'

'Right or left?'

The half-smile was still there. 'Whichever comes first. You won't get lost that way, Inspector, I promise you.'

Chapter Fifteen

'Of course I'll see the police, Sharon,' said Eric Paterson testily. 'Show them straight in.'

'Just a few questions, sir,' began Detective Inspector Sloan as the two policemen settled themselves down in the partners' room at the offices of Double Felix back in Berebury and Sharon speedily withdrew to her own room.

'That's what they always say, isn't it?' said Paterson, lifting a stack of files off a chair. He stood with them in his hands for a moment, looking for somewhere else to put them down. Finding nowhere at the right level, he eventually lowered the whole lot to the floor, where the individual files gradually canted over, ending up in a disordered heap.

'It's as good a beginning as any,' said Sloan philosophically.

'It's what Socrates said,' said Paterson grimly, 'and look where it got him. Now, what's this all about?'

'A missing goat—'

'You're joking, surely.' Paterson's expression was quite comical.

'No, sir. I'm quite serious. Did your partner happen to mention having heard it bleating when he was at the Minster last night?'

Paterson's brow went into deep furrows. 'Yes, he did, as it happens—'

'And did he mention it when he came in first thing?'

'Oh, yes.' Paterson nodded. 'To our secretary as well. That was before he went off to the hospital but I don't see what on earth—'

'And he also spoke of having seen two of the clergy over there . . .'

'That's right. The Bishop and the Dean,' said Paterson readily. 'Tell me, what has all this got to do with the police?'

'Just checking,' said Detective Inspector Sloan.

'That's something else they always say, isn't it?' said Paterson with twisted lips.

'It's something we always do,' said Detective Inspector Sloan with emphasis. 'Now I understand that your firm is about to do some work at Aumerle Court.'

'We are. My partner's been handling that, though.'

'If I might see the file . . .'

Eric Paterson pointed to the floor. 'We had it out this morning so it's one of those down on the dog shelf.' He stooped and started pulling the heap about. 'Here you are . . . Aumerle Court, marked for immediate action . . .'

'Plenty of that over there today,' said Crosby chattily.

Paterson gave the Constable a long, considering look. 'So I understand. All that Double Felix is meant to be doing at this stage is giving the owners the layout for installing the lighting for their project.' He shrugged his shoulders. 'I daresay I'll have to go over myself now that David is out of action.'

'Thank you, sir,' said Sloan, 'you've been very helpful. And if we might take the file away with us . . .'

Crosby clambered back into the driving seat of the police car and said 'Where to, now, sir?'

'The hospital,' said Sloan wearily. 'Let's go and see if we can make any sense out of whoever Master Bevis said he was with over there yesterday evening when he should have been at home with his missus.'

'Funny place to be carrying on with anyone,' said the Constable.

'Oh, I don't know,' mused Sloan. 'There's so much coming and going at hospitals that I should have thought you could have got away with murder without anyone noticing.' He fell silent for a moment. 'I dare say they're doing it all the time.'

'I shouldn't have wanted to have been at home myself with that Mrs Pedlinge anyway,' said Crosby frankly. 'All skin and bone and complaints.'

'An uncomfortable mixture,' agreed Sloan. 'Now, tell me what you made of the goat business—'

They were interrupted by a nasal voice on the car radio. 'Calling DI Sloan, calling DI Sloan of "F" Division . . .'

Sloan reached for the microphone and responded 'Go ahead.'

'A message, sir,' said the nasal voice, 'from the Superintendent. He said you were to be told at once that there is a Captain Jeremy Prosser here at the station wanting to make a statement in connection with the death of Margaret Collins.'

'Now, Miss Daphne, what have you been up to?' Milly Smithers came into the Long Gallery with a tea tray and took one look at her animated charge.

Daphne Pedlinge gave her a wolf-like smile. 'Sorting out Master Bevis, Milly, that's what I've been doing.'

'I can always tell when you've been up to something,' said Milly, setting down the tray on a long sideboard used for that purpose at the Court through many generations.

'Been wanting to do that for a long time,' cackled the old lady gleefully.

'It needed doing,' said Milly Smithers, who knew the Pedlinge family almost better than they knew themselves.

'Badly,' said Daphne Pedlinge. 'And', she said with considerable satisfaction, 'now I've done it.'

'Will it do any good, though?' asked Milly, who also had things riding on a substantial portion of the Pedlinge family money not being hived off to a disaffected wife. As jobs went these days, looking after Miss Daphne suited her down to the ground.

'Too soon to say, Milly,' she said, 'but he didn't like the idea of the police going off and talking to that Sister in the hospital who he says makes him feel better.' She gave a snort. 'Feel better! Where's his backbone? If Amanda won't act like a loving wife, then he should put his arms round her and give her a kiss and, if that doesn't work, then he should beat her.'

'I don't know why men play rugby,' said Milly with seeming irrelevance.

'Makes 'em feel bigger and stronger,' opined Miss Pedlinge. 'And it gave him a good excuse to go to the hospital. And keep going up there.'

'And she did kiss him better, I suppose,' said Milly cynically.

'The uniform helps,' said Daphne Pedlinge sagely. A distant look came into her eyes. 'Does a lot for a woman, a uniform.'

'And a man,' agreed Milly. 'Take my hubby, now. He's nothing in his old suit, but put him back in a uniform and he's a real man again.'

Daphne Pedlinge still had a faraway look in her eyes. 'An old wound . . .' She bit her lip and stopped. 'I mean an old injury . . . would have been the only excuse he needed.'

'What Master Bevis needs', said Milly Smithers firmly, 'is home comforts.'

'Which he hasn't got,' said Daphne Pedlinge. 'Not with Amanda.'

'He's let her get the upper hand,' said Milly, 'that's his trouble.' There had never been any such trouble in

159

the Smithers household. And while, had she known about it, Milly Smithers would undoubtedly have been all in favour of the Married Women's Property Act, she didn't hold with the idea of her son's wife getting a half-share in the bits and pieces she'd given him if the couple ever split up. Especially the pretty little china clock which had come to Milly from her own mother . . .

'I've sent him away with a flea in his ear,' said Daphne Pedlinge. 'No, not away. Home. And told him to stay there. The police can do their own detecting.' A shadow came over her face. 'Turns out, though, Milly, that Bevis knew this dead woman in the maze. And her husband. Worrying, that.'

'Don't you let that bother you, Miss Daphne,' said Milly Smithers robustly. 'There's more people know Tom Fool than Tom Fool knows.'

'That, Milly,' said Miss Daphne Pedlinge with some acerbity, 'is a great help, I must say.'

'There now,' said the woman, exercising the displacement skills shared by all carers, 'we're letting our egg get cold, aren't we?'

'Pah!' said Daphne Pedlinge.

The interview room at Berebury Staion was deliberately bare. There was a window, but it was high up in the wall and there was no view to be had from it. Also high up on the wall was a video camera and, on the wall opposite it, was a clock with a clear face.

The furniture was minimal – a small table and four chairs.

On two of these were sitting Captain Prosser and a middle-aged man, who introduced himself as the Captain's solicitor. 'I felt it appropriate in the circumstances, Inspector,' he said, 'having advised my client to make a statement, to accompany him while he did so.'

'We're ready when you are,' said Sloan, who was well aware why solicitors deemed it prudent to accompany their clients to the police station. This one was not local and thus a stranger to him.

Captain Prosser sat upright in his chair, looked straight ahead of him and said, 'I wish to state quite categorically that I did not have anything whatsoever to do with the death of Mrs Margaret Collins.'

'Make a note of that, Crosby,' said Sloan without any inflexion at all.

'Yes, sir.'

'I think my client might be a little more specific about his relationship with the deceased,' said the solicitor into the silence which followed.

The Captain flushed a deep red. 'I am prepared to admit that we knew each other very well.'

'Make a note of that, too,' said Sloan.

'I mean,' said the Captain, irritated, 'that we had had an affair.'

'But you're telling me now that it was all over long before she died, are you?' suggested Sloan genially. There were those in the Force who thought it rattling good sport to sit at the back of the Court and laugh aloud at the evidence of the accused, but Sloan was not one of them. There were other ways of casting doubt on what was said by the guilty, but only after that guilt had been firmly established and not before. Fair was fair, even at the police station.

'Yes.'

'How long ago?'

'About six months.'

'Might I ask when and how it terminated?' Every policeman knew that it was the end of the affair that was the moment of danger. Usually for the woman. But not always.

Captain Prosser didn't hesitate. 'The day after James's eye condition was diagnosed we broke it off—'

'We?' echoed Sloan gently.

'She—' said Prosser.

'I see.' And Sloan thought he did.

'She – Margaret – said that there was no room in her life just then for anything but James.' He licked his lips. 'I could understand that and we stopped seeing each other except when I met the Collinses socially in Nether Hoystings. We remained neighbours, of course.'

'But you were still seeing her husband at Aumerle Court, too.'

Prosser relaxed a fraction. 'Oh, yes. That was no problem. I'd always known David as well as Margaret and Double Felix is a very good firm. The best.'

'And how did he feel about being cuckolded?' asked

Detective Inspector Sloan. If there was one thing for sure, it was that Crosby wouldn't know how to spell the word, still less remember its meaning.

Captain Prosser understood what he meant all right. 'I have no reason to think that David knew about our affair,' he said stiffly. 'Margaret said she was sure he didn't. We were always very discreet. For James's sake.'

'This affair,' said Detective Inspector Sloan, trying to keep what he thought about affairs with married women out of his tone, 'how long had it lasted?'

Captain Prosser shot a swift glance in the direction of his solicitor, who nodded almost imperceptibly. 'About three years,' he replied uneasily.

'And James is – let me see now . . .' murmured Sloan. It had once been a cardinal principle of English law that children born within wedlock were the sons and daughters of the husband of the marriage, but now a mysterious substance called deoxyribonucleic acid had upset all that. DNA and genetic fingerprinting had taken over and you were what the results of those tests said you were. He, Sloan, didn't know whether that was good or bad, but as someone else had said, 'A man's a man for all that.'

'Two,' said Prosser shortly.

'So . . .'

'I have no actual reason to suppose that James is my son,' said the Captain. 'Nor did Margaret ever suggest otherwise to me, but . . . .', he swallowed, 'the trouble is we couldn't be absolutely sure.'

163

Detective Inspector Sloan wasn't listening. He was trying to remember what Dr Chomel had told him about the difficulties of the genetic counselling of parents of children with retinoblastoma without a full DNA analysis. And Dr Browne had said something important, too. He must check on that as well.

'No reason whatsoever,' repeated Prosser.

Sloan still wasn't listening.

He was thinking that David Collins, though, might well have excellent grounds for not just thinking but being absolutely sure that little James was not his son.

Which was something very different.

Chapter Sixteen

'You've arrested Prosser, I take it, Sloan,' said Superintendent Leeyes.

'No, sir.'

'I've said before and I'll say it again, Sloan, that you're not quick enough off the mark in the way of arrests.' The Superintendent's eyebrows came together in a ferocious glare. 'The fact that he'd got his solicitor with him shouldn't have made any difference at all. You've only got to go by the book and you're all right.'

'It wasn't that . . .'

'Did he have an alibi for yesterday evening, then?' He grunted. 'Granted you've got to check that out first or we'll have the human rights people round our necks.'

'No, sir, as it happened he didn't.' Sloan wasn't quite sure where human rights came into the frame – or whether they should be lumped with all the other do-gooders the Superintendent so disliked – but he did know that Leeyes was all against them whenever they did crop up. 'Captain Prosser tells me that he went for a good long walk over the Bield after Aumerle Court closed for the day.' The Bield was a low mound, criss-crossed with footpaths not far from Berebury Golf Course.

'What he tells you, Sloan, isn't evidence until it's proved.'

'He says he went alone and saw no one except for a few golfers leaving the clubhouse as he came down the path off the Bield that's near the eighteenth fairway.'

'And did they see him?' asked Leeyes pertinently.

'He doesn't know – the last of the light had nearly gone by then.'

'At least the husband's got an impeccable alibi,' grunted the Superintendent. 'Even in this secular day and age, the word of a Bishop and a Dean should carry some weight.'

'And a goat . . .'

'What's that, Sloan? What's that?' The Superintendent frowned. 'Where does a goat come in?'

'I only wish I knew,' said Detective Inspector Sloan, rising to his feet. 'I'll get back to you as soon as I can, sir.'

He left the Superintendent's room and was making his way back to his own when he encountered his old friend, Inspector Harpe from Traffic Division, in the corridor. 'Just the man I wanted to see, Harry.'

'What about?' asked that worthy cautiously. He was known as Happy Harry throughout the Calleshire Constabulary because he had never been seen to smile. For his part he maintained that there had never

ever been anything in Traffic Division at which to so much as twitch one's lips, let alone smile. 'If it's about that Constable of yours wanting to transfer to Traffic you can forget it. He only gets to come over my bod deady. Understood?'

'Understood,' said Sloan pacifically. 'No, Harry, I was wondering what you thought the odds are on whether a van could be driven from Calleford to Staple St James and back without being seen after dark.'

'And parked?'

'Yes.'

'How long parked for?'

Sloan leaned back on his heels and thought. 'Long enough for a man to trundle an industrial-sized rubbish bin all the way round a maze, tip a woman's body out in the exact middle and retrace his steps to his vehicle.'

'No.'

'No what?'

'No way that it could be done without somebody spotting it somewhere.' He hunched his shoulders. 'Especially when it was parked. Seeing unfamiliar vehicles in unfamiliar places seems to bring out something primitive in people.'

'This was a Sunday evening.'

'Then they'd have been even more likely to notice a commercial vehicle,' said Happy Harry. 'By the way, how did your chummie get to the middle of a maze in the dark? I can never do it even in daylight.'

* * * * *

Detective Constable Crosby was in Sloan's office when he got back there. 'Your wife rang, sir, while you were out. She wants to know when you're coming home. If you are, that is.'

Sloan sat down and pushed his hands through his hair. 'Might as well go home,' he said, 'for all the good we're doing here. It's getting late, anyway.'

'She said, sir, to say she wondered', continued Crosby, unsure of the wisdom of delivering this part of her message, 'if you were ever coming home again.'

Sloan gave a great yawn. 'I am, but before I went home I had wanted to work out who it is who had killed Mrs Margaret Collins and why.'

'And how they did it, sir. Don't forget that.'

'We know how, Crosby. You know that. Dr Dabbe said she died from an overdose of a sedative called Crespusculan. How she ingested it, of course, is for us to establish.' The Crown Prosecution Service would want them to prove beyond reasonable doubt that it wasn't by accident, but that would have to wait. 'Me, I reckon she was slipped a Mickey Finn.' He grimaced. 'Always plenty of those around at the hospital, too, as well as in the home as in her case . . .'

'I didn't mean that sort of how, sir.' Crosby screwed up his face in an effort to express himself better. 'I meant how did whoever kill her get her to where she was found in the dark. She wasn't going to walk in there herself if she wasn't planning on committing . . . what is it they call suicide now?'

'Voluntary death, but what's in a name, Crosby?'

'You tell me, sir.'

'I reckon she went in inside one of those big bins, all right.' He pushed his notebook away. 'Forensic think they'll be able to confirm that by morning.'

'I didn't mean that either,' Crosby said awkwardly. 'I meant how did whoever did it get about in the maze in the dark, let alone to the very centre. Light from a torch would have shown up and, for all the murderer knew, the old lady at the window would have spotted that.'

'True, very true.' Sloan gave another, even bigger yawn. 'Perhaps', he said lightly, 'he used a ball of wool like that lady statue. Ariadne, did Miss Pedlinge say she was called . . .' He sat up, his tiredness dropping away. 'A good length of string would have done, Crosby, wouldn't it?'

'Yes, sir.'

'The only person in the maze with a reason for using string or anything else like it to measure the maze was David Collins.'

'Who was measuring up for Double Felix's estimate,' said Crosby, light dawning.

'Before their very eyes, so to speak, although', said Sloan fairly, 'anyone else could have seen that it was there, too, and used it. Or brought their own.'

'Collins was the only one who could count on it being there, though,' pointed out Crosby.

'And David Collins is the only one with a solid alibi,' said Sloan ruefully. 'I ask you, Crosby, a Bishop and a Dean . . .'

'And a goat, called Aries,' put in Crosby, 'which he told everyone he'd heard and which he couldn't have done if he hadn't been there.'

Detective Inspector Sloan pulled his notebook back towards him. 'Not so fast, m'lad. He could still have told everyone he'd heard it even if it hadn't been there, couldn't he? Just you take another look at what the goat lady said, will you?'

The Detective Constable leafed through his own notebook. 'She thought she would have noticed if Aries had been missing at the seven-thirty feed, but she couldn't swear to him having been there.'

'The goat could have been stolen later on in the night – nobody else said they heard him until this morning.' Sloan flung his pen down on his desk. 'It doesn't get us anywhere, though. At the time Collins was miles away from where the action was to boot and he couldn't have got there by walking. He had to have pushed the body up to the Minotaur before Milly Smithers locked the postern gate.' He must be more tired than he had realized if he had taken to mixing metaphors like this. 'Inspector Harpe is finding out if anyone on duty in Traffic saw a Double Felix van anywhere on Sunday evening except at the Close, where the Security people say it was all evening, but I'm not very hopeful. Murderers don't drive around with vans with their names on.'

'You'd have thought that fellow Bevis Pedlinge could have done better than saying he'd driven over to the hospital, but that the sister he's sweet on was off-duty, wouldn't you, sir?'

'I'm not sure which is best, Crosby, no alibi like Jeremy Prosser, half an alibi like Bevis Pedlinge or a rock-solid one like the man Collins.' Perhaps the Superintendent hadn't been so far off the mark as Sloan had thought when he'd quoted that old choosing chant 'Eenie, meanie, miney, mo'. 'By the way, Crosby, Inspector Harpe tells me that he's had a complaint from the rider of a Harley-Davidson about being cut up by a speeding police car.'

'Some people can't take a joke,' responded Crosby heatedly. 'You can't tell what a man's like under one of those great crash helmets, let alone who he is . . .'

Sloan went suddenly still. 'Suppose – just suppose, Crosby – that Collins had gone from the Minster at Calleford to Aumerle Court by motorcycle after the vehicle gates had closed and got in through that little postern gate and then pushed his wife round to the maze, tipped her out, replaced the bin in the bothy, and gone back to the Minster. Who would have noticed?'

'The Bishop and the Dean,' said Crosby promptly. 'He wouldn't have been there to have been seen when he was.'

'Motorcycle leathers are as good a disguise as any, though,' Sloan was saying as the telephone rang.

'For you, sir,' said Crosby. 'It's Mrs Sloan. She's wondering if you've forgotten where you live.'

'"Show me the way to go home . . ."' hummed Sloan. 'Tell her I'm on my way.'

He noticed Crosby's face suddenly turn pink with

171

pleasure as he replaced the telephone receiver. 'She's asked me, too, sir. It's Lancashire hotpot for supper.'

The telephone rang late, too, in a modest house in Nether Hoystings.

'That you, David?' said Eric Paterson. 'I just thought I'd better see how things were over there.'

'Pretty bloody,' said David Collins. 'Margaret's mother thought it was as well to take James straight back with her from the hospital.'

'Less upsetting for the little chap than coming home and then leaving again,' agreed Paterson.

'I've just had a policewoman here calling herself the family liaison officer, but she's gone again. Not that she could tell me anything much . . .'

'No . . .'

'And now the house feels emptier than ever. If you must know, Eric, I've just had the biggest whisky I could swallow.'

'Don't blame you.'

'Everyone's been very kind,' he said savagely, 'which they think helps and, let me tell you, it doesn't. Not one little bit. In fact,' he hiccuped, 'it makes everything even worse.'

'You'll get some sleep on the whisky, anyway,' said Paterson.

'Sleep!' he echoed. 'Believe you me, Eric, I've never felt less like sleep in my entire life.'

'I quite understand,' said his partner peaceably. 'But even so, you won't feel like work tomorrow and I need to know the state of play with one or two projects, so as to keep things going.'

'Let me think a minute – so much has happened since this morning. Well, I finished at the Minster, except for the new work they talked about this morning, which'll need sorting.'

'Right.'

'All the equipment's in the van.' He gulped. 'I'd just finished tidying up and loading when the police came for me there to say about Margaret's having been . . .' He swallowed audibly. 'To tell me about Margaret.'

'The police came to us for your file on Aumerle Court this afternoon,' said Eric Paterson quietly.

'What's that got to do with them . . .?' His voice fell away. 'Oh, the maze . . . yes, I'd started to measure that up. God, I never thought of that.'

'They did.'

'They would.' He groaned. 'Listen, Eric, I swear that I didn't know my way around the place and how Margaret did beats me . . .' His voice trailed away. 'What a ghastly business it all is.'

'Yes,' agreed Paterson.

He gave another little hiccup. 'And it's no use your saying I'll feel better in the morning, Eric, because I know I shan't.'

'I know you won't, too, David. From where I sit there's a lot more to come on this and none of it'll be good.'

He didn't add that it wouldn't be good for Double Felix Ltd, either, but he thought it.

Mary Wallingford's bedtime routine was every bit as ritualized as her husband's saying of his daily Office. Whereas the Bishop was a man who got speedily into bed, his wife pottered round the bedroom, gradually shedding her involvement with the day as she worked her way slowly through the nightly business of undressing, washing, brushing her hair and applying various unguents to her face.

'Bertie . . .', she said, still sitting at her dressing table.

'Yes, m'dear?' He didn't look up from his favourite bedtime reading.

'Bertie, I suppose you're quite sure you saw David Collins working in the slype last night—'

'Well, if it wasn't him, then it was somebody very like him and there was nobody else with any reason to be there.'

'There wasn't really a lot of reason for him to be there either,' she said.

'The clergy aren't the only people who are busy on Sundays, you know,' he said, turning over another page of his well-worn Zane Grey. 'Quite a lot of people work then. More than ever before, actually, these days.'

'Malby saw him, too, didn't he?' she said uncertainly.

'He did.'

She laid down her hairbrush. 'Bertie, I don't like what's going on in the Close.'

'I can't say I do either, m'dear.'

'Don't forget "Sticks and stones may break our bones",' she said. 'And there were sticks and stones on our step as well as those other things.'

'You musn't lose your sense of proportion, Mary. It's nothing compared with what some people have to put up with and it's nothing that can't be taken care of, either.'

'You don't think there's someone out there who might have driven poor Margaret Collins to take her own life with all this black magic – somebody with a grudge, perhaps . . .'

'Perhaps, but we must be rational about it.'

She paused in the brushing of her hair, her hand suspended above her head. 'I'm worried that it might turn even nastier.'

'Have faith – and for Heaven's sake woman, come and get into bed.'

Chapter Seventeen

Tuesdays, or rather this Tuesday, showed every sign of not being a good-hair day at the Berebury Police Station any more than the Monday had been. For one thing, Superintendent Leeyes wanted an immediate update on the death of Margaret Collins. As soon as Detective Inspector Sloan came in, anyway. If not sooner. There was a terse message to this effect waiting on his desk when the head of Berebury's tiny Criminal Investigation Department reached it the next morning.

There was also the first of a stream of reports. Forensic had found hairs and what they euphemistically described as 'body fluids' inside one of the waste bins in the bothy. The hair matched that of the deceased. There had been no fingerprints on the bin handle other than those of Kenny Prickett, but there were signs of the handle previously having been wiped suspiciously clean. Dyson and Williams had sent over a set of official photographs which, though not pretty, showed the body of the deceased from every possible angle. They'd sent some unofficial pictures, too, of the statue of the Minotaur taken from several unexpected aspects.

'Who do they think they are?' grumbled Sloan, unamused. 'Man Ray?'

'Comes of watching too many wildlife programmes,' said Crosby.

The Sister on the twilight shift at the Accident and Emergency Department at the hospital had been interviewed and agreed that, since they asked, she often spent time with Bevis Pedlinge on Sunday evenings – and a great many other weekend evenings when on duty, which she hadn't been this Sunday – dating from the time he had first attended some months ago with a minor injury and a deeply troubled mind.

She had variously prescribed marital counselling, anti-depressants, emigration, referral to a psychotherapist, trial separation and – as a last resort – she had suggested the socks treatment . . .

'What's that, sir?' asked Crosby when he came upon it in the written record.

'It's like shock treatment, Crosby, except that you do it yourself.'

He frowned. 'Socks treatment?'

'Pulling them up,' said Sloan. 'Although I don't know that I'd care to be caught between the two ladies in his life myself.' The Greeks had had a word – or, rather, two words – for Bevis Pedlinge's situation. They were Scylla and Charybdis. 'Two lots of great – and very different – expectations are a bit much for a young man like him. No wonder he's taken to writing

177

pageants. Amateur dramatics can get a lot out of the system.'

'There's this follow-up on Captain Prosser, too,' said Crosby, picking up another report. 'He's got a right old nosey parker for a next-door neighbour – the sort that counts the handkerchiefs on the washing line and asks if you've got a cold.'

'A very present help in time of trouble to an investigating officer,' said Sloan. 'Tell me more.'

'She says she'd always thought he'd had a little piece on the side, but she'd never been able to find out who the lady in question was.'

'A very discreet man, our Captain Prosser.'

'And Mrs Collins must have been a discreet woman,' said Crosby. 'Especially if the husband didn't know either. Or anyone else, come to that.'

'It can be done,' growled Sloan. 'They say it adds to the excitement.'

'Myself, I wouldn't know, sir.'

'I should hope not,' said Sloan.

'Anyway, she says it shook Prosser rigid to get the chop as estate manager at the Earl of Ornum's place. According to this old biddy next door, he's been on the straight and narrow ever since.'

'By "straight and narrow", does she mean no love life at all?' enquired Sloan with interest. They had criminals on their books at the police station who didn't equate being on the straight and narrow with marital fidelity at all. Not for a moment. On the contrary, sometimes.

'She does. At least,' said Crosby, scanning the report, 'none that she has seen. No one answering to the description of Margaret Collins ever came to his house alone that she saw – she knew her well by sight anyway, being a neighbour. She was quite sure about that.'

'A careful man, our Captain Prosser.' He tapped the desk with his pencil. 'We're looking for a careful man, Crosby, don't forget. A very careful man.'

'A very clever man, too,' said the Constable morosely. 'The people on the Ornum estate knew he had been seeing a married woman, but didn't know who she was either. They said the Earl didn't like it.'

Sloan couldn't remember the family motto of the Earls of Ornum – or how many Countesses the current one had had – but the motto had something to do with fealty, forbearance and fortitude. He must look it up sometime – especially fealty.

'The child's diagnosis could have been the catalyst for the end of the affair,' he said to Crosby. 'Not the loss of the job, although no one would guess.'

'Yes, sir.' Crosby laid the report down. 'But Prosser's not going to kill the woman now for ending it for whatever. Not after all this time, surely?'

'There is a quotation that all police officers ignore at their peril, Crosby.'

'Sir?'

'It goes something like "Revenge is a dish that can be eaten cold."'

'Yes, sir.'

'But', sighed Sloan, 'I do have to say that I myself

saw Prosser recognize the deceased in the maze through Miss Pedlinge's binoculars and I could swear he was genuinely surprised and shocked at the sight, for all his Army discipline and training in self-control.'

'If it's David Collins after all,' sniffed Crosby, 'then he managed to push that bin into the maze at exactly the same moment as he was being seen by the Bishop and the Dean miles away.'

'As alibis go,' conceded Detective Inspector Sloan with a sigh, 'being seen by a Dean and a Bishop takes a lot of beating.'

'He could have met his wife as she left the hospital without anyone spotting her, though,' Crosby flipped over his notebook, 'because they've got that little "live waiting" area for cars at the side. We've got someone asking if either of them were seen in the car park, naturally, but no joy on that yet.'

'Remember, for all anyone else knows, she might never have intended to stay overnight there at all, Crosby.' Sloan thought for a moment. 'The husband could have given her the sedative in a cup of tea from the Thermos that he said he had in the van and, when she'd dozed off, driven over to Aumerle Court with her unconscious—'

'But that doesn't help, sir,' objected Crosby.

'Oh, yes, it does,' responded Sloan. 'All he has to do, then, is to back his van up against the bothy, open the doors and decant her into one of the bins . . .'

'And go off and measure up the maze with Bevis

Pedlinge and Captain Prosser, do you mean?' asked Crosby.

'Exactly. The body would be safe enough in the bin until it was dark,' said Sloan. 'Do you remember Kenny Prickett telling us they didn't work Sundays any more? Don't forget, the Captain put a stop to overtime when he came.'

'All right, then, so Collins goes over to the Minster at Calleford, leaving the body in a bin, lays a trail under the noses of the other two men to get back through the maze, pretending it's for an estimate from his firm – then what, sir?'

'Aye, Crosby,' said Sloan, pushing his own notebook away and sitting back. 'Then what? That's where we come to a full stop. Collins is over at the Minster at the material time and the body of his wife is at Aumerle Court.'

Sloan sat silently for a moment, his mind somewhere else. What was it that Miss Pedlinge had said was the way out of the maze? He tried to remember. Advance right up to every dead end before backtracking and only backtrack as far as the next opening – the first on either side. That was it. Then take that route and do the same again until you get out of the maze. He nodded to himself, staring down at his notes. This case would make a good parallel with her theory – at least they had advanced up to plenty of dead ends in it, met them and retreated.

The goat wasn't a dead end.

The goat was an unsolved mystery.

'Have a word with Calleford, Crosby, and check whether they've been having any black mass trouble in a wider area over there, will you? Ought to have done it before, I suppose.'

'Can't think of everything,' said that worthy blithely.

'That's just where're you're wrong, Crosby,' he said sternly. 'You have to in this job, and the sooner you realize that the better.'

'Yes, sir,' Crosby said with unusual meekness. 'What exactly am I checking?'

'When all this nonsense with rabbit's bones and pentagrams started and whether anyone else heard the goat bleating while Collins was there on Sunday evening. The Bishop said he didn't.'

'The Bishop's wife heard it the next morning,' the Constable said.

'That's different.' Sloan sat up. 'And your goat lady didn't miss Aries until the morning, did she?'

'Not for certain.' Crosby wrinkled his brow. 'All she said was that she thought she would have missed Aries if he hadn't been there.'

'Suppose', said Sloan slowly, 'the goat hadn't been put into the Canon's garden until much later—'

'Then David Collins couldn't have heard it,' said Crosby, puzzled. 'But he said he heard it.'

'Exactly, Crosby. He said he heard it, but we don't know for certain that he did. We have no real proof that he heard it or that anyone else did until the next day, have we?'

'We don't need proof, do we, sir? We already know that David Collins was there then. The Bishop and the Dean saw him.'

'Or someone impersonating him.' As Detective Inspector Sloan pushed his hands against the edges of his desk to get to his feet, his telephone rang.

Detective Constable Crosby picked it up.

'It's the Superintendent, sir,' he said to Sloan. 'He wants to see you now.'

'Milly, are you there?'

'Yes, Miss Daphne, I'm here. Is there something you want?'

'Milly, I'm a daft old woman who's lived too long.'

'No, you're not, Miss Daphne,' said the carer stoutly.

'And I should have been dead years ago. Easier for everyone.'

'No, you shouldn't, Miss Daphne.'

'I've been very silly.'

'Not you . . .'

'Yes, me. I should have realized that everything was getting too much for Master Bevis.'

'He's still young,' said Milly indulgently.

'Young?' Daphne Pedlinge almost reared up in her wheelchair. 'Why, when I was half his age—'

'That's part of the problem, Miss Daphne.' Milly Smithers struggled to put her thoughts into acceptable words. 'You'd grown up – had to, more's the pity – by the time you were as old as Master Bevis is now.'

The old woman grunted.

'He's still a little boy who wants everyone to be happy,' said Milly.

'He's let everything get him down,' snorted the old lady unsympathetically. 'And that's no good in this life. It doesn't do, you know. No matter what.'

'Master Bevis doesn't know yet that everyone can't all be happy. Not at the same time, anyway. Specially that Amanda.'

'Hrmmph. As for Amanda . . .'

'I dare say', said Milly percipiently, 'when he married her he thought she was just a bit of fluff and she isn't.'

'She's pure steel,' said the pot, paying due tribute to the kettle.

'There you are, then,' said Milly. 'You don't really think he had anything to do with the dead woman in the maze, do you, Miss Daphne?'

'Certainly not. He wouldn't hurt a fly,' said his great-aunt, spoiling any suspicion of benevolence by adding, 'that's his trouble.'

'We're just checking on one or two points, miss,' said Detective Inspector Sloan to Sharon Gibbons when he and Crosby got to the offices of Double Felix Ltd. 'Going over the same ground again, you might say.' In a bruising encounter with him before he had left the police station, Superintendent Leeyes had called the proposed interview something very different when

Sloan had suggested it. But he did not mention this to the secretary.

'I'm afraid there's nobody here but me,' she said apologetically. 'Poor David isn't coming in today, of course, and Eric's gone over to Aumerle Court to see what he can do about their sound and lighting production instead. Time's getting very short, you see, and it's important.'

'So it's quite soon, is it, miss, this effort of theirs?'

She nodded. 'It's already being heavily advertised, that's the trouble. "A Pageant of Light", it's called. David had naturally done a lot of the work beforehand, that is before . . .' Her voice fell away and she became silent.

'What sort of work?' he asked encouragingly. As things stood, the Criminal Investigation Department of 'F' Division at Berebury was interested in anything – but anything – that David Collins had done at Aumerle Court beforehand or not.

She stared at Sloan. 'Why, designing and preparing the lighting circuits, of course. And setting them up. That's his job.'

'I'm afraid, miss, I don't understand your sort of thing.' In a lifetime in the Police Force Sloan had always found a statement of ignorance – genuine or assumed – to be a very real help. 'Tell me what it's all about.'

Sharon Gibbons sat back, ready to explain exactly what it was that Double Felix did. Her own mother didn't quite understand either, so she chose her words with care. 'We make lighting do what we want,' she said with a simplicity which would have appealed to Michael Faraday himself. 'You know, bend it, throw it about, make it come up here and there.' She looked from Sloan's deliberately uncomprehending face to Crosby's genuinely uninterested one and tried again. 'Make things seem to be there when they're not really . . . if you understand.'

'I understand,' breathed Detective Inspector Sloan.

'They're going to have a pretend Cavalier . . .' Sharon warmed to her theme as Sloan got to his feet. 'And a Roundhead . . .'

'Come along, Crosby,' he commanded.

'It's called a hologram,' she called out after them.

But the two policemen had gone and, just like the characters in Shakespeare's play *Macbeth*, they had not stood upon the order of their going.

Chapter Eighteen

'And he didn't resist arrest?' enquired Superintendent Leeyes with professional interest.

'He came very quietly,' said Detective Inspector Sloan.

'That can be a bad sign, Sloan.'

'Yes, sir, I know.' It wasn't a case of 'eenie, meanie, miney, mo' any longer. Not now he knew exactly how David Collins could for all intents and purposes have appeared to have been in one place when at the same time he had actually been somewhere else.

'Did he say anything?' The Superintendent was a great believer in noting down the first response of the accused to a charge: usually to be used in evidence against them.

'He seemed resigned – no, that's the wrong word, sir.' He frowned. 'More satisfied.'

'Satisfied that he'd killed his wife?'

'Yes, sir.'

'Because she'd had an affair?'

Sloan shook his head. 'No, no, sir. Not just for that. I don't mean that that's insufficient reason,' he added hastily, since the Superintendent's views on the sanctity of marriage were widely known. Or, perhaps, they were his wife's views . . .

'What then?' Leeyes sniffed.

'For making him have a vasectomy in case he carried a gene for the child's condition, when he wasn't the father of the child concerned.'

The Superintendent leaned back in his chair and puffed out his cheeks. 'As motives for murder go, Sloan,' he said judiciously, 'it would command a lot of sympathy from a male jury.'

'It's as good as any I've met,' agreed Detective Inspector Sloan, husband and parent.

'He wasn't tempted to make away with Captain Prosser as well, do you suppose?'

'We can't be absolutely sure of this, sir, but it is entirely possible that Collins didn't know that Prosser was the father of James.' Sloan flipped over a page in his notebook. 'According to the interviews we've conducted, the only genetic information that Collins can possibly have been given was that he was not the father of James. Not who was.'

'It's a wise child who knows its own father,' observed the Superintendent.

'Obviously the tests don't extend as far as that and Prosser is adamant that Collins didn't know he was the guilty party.' He looked up. 'Their continued working and social relationship would tend to confirm that.'

'No struggle, then?' The Superintendent sounded disappointed.

'No, sir.' A struggle and a heated denial – or better still, the spilling of beans – were seen as welcome indicators of guilt by some law enforcers. 'As I said, he came very quietly.'

'You're quite sure of your case, I hope, Sloan?'

'Quite sure, sir.'

'And the charade with the Minotaur over at Aumerle Court?'

'Miss Daphne, I mean Miss Pedlinge, explained that. It was part of his plan to make his wife's death seem like suicide as well as creating a time-frame. So was the nearly empty cup of sedative. Reaching the centre of the maze is a metaphor for death.'

Leeyes grunted.

'And if he hadn't bumped her face on the stone as he laid her there, he might well have got away with it.' Detective Inspector Sloan, upholder of the law, had to admit this.

'Manhandling an unconscious woman takes a bit of doing,' agreed Leeyes as if it was something he did every day. 'How did you say Collins rigged his famous alibi over at Calleford?'

'In several ways, sir. Firstly, he said he had seen the Bishop and the Dean walking past, talking together, after Evensong.'

'Not unlikely that they would, I suppose,' admitted Leeyes grudgingly.

'They'd done it every Sunday since the Dean lost his wife and the Bishop's wife gave him supper. I expect Collins had checked on this. Then Collins

189

mentioned to his partner that he'd heard a goat bleating when he hadn't actually tethered the goat there until much later on in the night. Nobody else heard it until the morning, but the presumption was that he and the goat had both been there earlier.'

'Can't abide goats myself,' said Leeyes irrelevantly. 'And what else?'

'A very clever set-up indeed, sir. He fixed up a hologram image of himself just inside the entrance to the slype at the Minster, working off a time-switch.'

'Ah, a hologram.' The Superintendent nodded sagely. 'Tell me, how precisely will you explain that to the Crown Prosecution Service?'

'Easy, sir.' He grinned. 'As a way of producing with laser beams a three-dimensional image that isn't there.' The Crown Prosecution Service probably wouldn't need it explaining to them. He was prepared to bet, though, that the Superintendent did. He coughed. 'DC Crosby came quite near to guessing the answer early on.'

'Crosby?' echoed Leeyes in patent disbelief.

'He suggested that it had been done with mirrors.' For a delicious moment Sloan toyed with the idea of saying that this reflected great credit on Crosby, too, but decided against it. Instead he went on, 'Collins, who is, of course, a very highly skilled lighting engineer, set up the hologram gear on the Sunday after he'd dumped his unconscious wife over at Aumerle Court and on the Monday morning he dismantled it all, loaded the equipment on to his van and took it away again under everyone's eyes.'

'I suppose there was no one there who would have recognized it anyway, if they had happened to spot it,' said Leeyes loftily.

'Almost certainly not for what it was, if they had,' agreed Sloan. 'The firm of Double Felix had been asked to put lighting in that area anyway, and I doubt if anyone at the Minster would have suspected anything.'

'In my experience', said the Superintendent largely, 'the clergy aren't good with material things.'

'No, sir.'

The clergy were good on logic, though.

Very good.

'I take it, Inspector,' said the Bishop a little later, 'that the – er – unChristian intrusions into the gardens in the Close were part and parcel of the man's attempt to establish an alibi – the pentagram, dead rabbit and so forth?'

'Yes, sir,' said Sloan.

'And the goat?'

'That, too. We reckon that this was all a meticulously planned affair. He starts to distribute all these symbolic . . . er . . . anti-Christian artefacts around the Close a week or so earlier so that you would take action on the assumption that some group or other was attacking the Church . . .'

'I'm afraid that does happen from time to time, Inspector,' said Bertram Wallingford gravely.

'Which strengthened the likelihood of your getting something more done about the lighting,' said Sloan.

'True.' The Bishop gazed round the ancient Close. 'I fear that this man Collins must have felt a very deep hatred of his wife to have done all this, not in the heat of the moment, so to speak, but after much thought and calculation.'

'He did,' said Sloan simply.

'And at a time when his child was so ill. My wife knew all about that from the nursery school, you know.' He looked across the Close. 'I'm sorry she's not here now, but she's just gone out to buy me a new dressing gown.'

'I'm afraid the illness had something to do with it,' said Sloan. 'We're only just beginning to put the whole story together, but we think that James's illness was the catalyst . . .' He stopped. 'No, not the catalyst – that's when something happens that leaves the agent of change unchanged itself, isn't it?'

'It is.' Bertram Wallingford said, 'I think the word you may be looking for is synergist. Where the combined action of the parts is greater than the sum of the individual parts and both are changed in the process.'

'Then I'm not sure,' Sloan said honestly.

'I thought that was the marriage value,' put in Detective Constable Crosby unexpectedly.

'Anyway,' Sloan struggled to get back to the matter in hand, 'the significant thing was that James's particular illness can have an hereditary component . . .'

'So my wife tells me,' said the Bishop. 'She'd taken

192

an interest in the family since she heard about his eye.'

'As a consequence of which', continued Sloan carefully, 'David Collins took steps to see that he didn't have any more children.' The Greeks probably had a word for this: Shakespeare had simply caused Richard III to declare among his other physical deficiencies, 'I, that am rudely stamp'd, and want love's majesty', which was explicit enough.

The Bishop of Calleford nodded. 'That is quite understandable in the circumstances.'

'But,' plodded on Sloan, 'in the course of James's treatment he then found out quite conclusively that he wasn't James's father.'

The Bishop raised both his hands in front of him in a gesture that might have been a blessing. 'That would be a very difficult one for any man – especially a husband – to live with,' he conceded.

'It seems that the parents had both gone in for some genetic testing after the child's diagnosis had been made and this got married up with the results of some similar examinations the hospital had done on the boy.' Detective Inspector Sloan had moved from considering a little learning being a bad thing, to deciding that even more learning was an even worse thing. Medical science and doctors could go too far.

'That was when the situation changed, I take it?' said Bertram Wallingford quietly.

'And the rot set in,' supplemented Crosby.

The Bishop of Calleford said almost petulantly, 'I do

wish people would leave vengeance to the Lord. The Bible tells us clearly that it is His. Quite clearly.'

'So, Inspector,' concluded the old lady at Aumerle Court, 'my great-nephew was simply not up to the pressures of today and sought consolation elsewhere.'

'They don't make them like they used to, Miss Pedlinge,' said the policeman.

'True, very true.' She swung her wheelchair away from him and stared out at the maze. 'And I should therefore be tempering the wind to the shorn lamb, should I? Is that what you're saying?'

'To two shorn lambs, madam . . .'

'I beg your pardon?'

'I think you will find your agent a somewhat chastened man.'

'Ha! So he comes into this debacle, too, does he?'

'We don't know to what extent and he declines to tell us anything more.'

'At least one person round here can keep their mouth shut—'

'Now, Miss Daphne . . .' began Milly Smithers.

'But there is a rumour going around,' said Sloan carefully, 'just a rumour, mind you, that Captain Prosser has made himself responsible for the expenses of little James Collins's upbringing.'

Detective Inspector Sloan found himself the recipient of prolonged scrutiny from a pair of shrewd old eyes. 'That, Inspector, is what I would call really confusing the issue.' She gave a high cackle.

'In both senses,' agreed Sloan appreciatively.

'So I've got to be kind to him, too, have I?'

'Now, Miss Daphne,' said Milly Smithers, 'there's no call for you to get excited.'

'More's the pity,' said the figure in the wheelchair.

Eric Paterson swung round on his swivel chair at the offices of Double Felix to face the two policemen. 'I was beginning to wonder about David myself, Inspector, and then when Sharon told me you'd taken off at the mere mention of holograms, I guessed, too.'

'If you would explain a little more about them it might help,' said Sloan.

'I'll say,' said Crosby.

Paterson tilted his chair back. 'It's essentially a photograph produced without a lens, by the interference between two split laser beams, which . . . oh, good, coffee. Thanks, Sharon . . . sugar, anyone?'

'No, thanks.'

'Yes, please.'

'Where was I?'

'With two split laser beams,' said Sloan.

Paterson carried on, 'Which, when suitably illuminated, shows a three-dimensional image which you can design yourself, of course.'

'Well, I never,' said Crosby. 'Got a spoon, anyone?'

'But', admitted Paterson, 'I would never have

195

worked out why he did it. He never gave anyone a clue how he really felt about Margaret.'

'Everyone was playing their cards very close to their chests,' said Sloan.

'Especially him,' said Crosby. He drained his coffee. 'We don't know when he found out about his wife having had an affair, of course.'

'Someone had got a dead man's hand, all right,' said Paterson. 'Or don't you play poker?'

'Not as a game,' said Sloan sedately. The poker the police played was of quite a different variety.

Paterson jerked his head. 'When do we get to get our van back?'

Constable Crosby came into his own at last. 'When we've checked the oil on the inside back floor with that in the motorbike Collins had hidden in it to get from Calleford to Aumerle Court and back. Those little machines may not be Harley-Davidsons but they aren't at all bad.'

'And the beauty of it,' said Sloan, mindful of his friend from Traffic Division, 'is that you can never see who's on them when they're wearing leathers and a crash helmet.'

'You can get away with murder then,' added Crosby, stirring his coffee.

'Not quite,' said Detective Inspector Sloan, closing his notebook with a snap. He permitted himself a wry smile. 'Not now we've seen the light.'